A MALLORCAN SUMMER OF SECOND CHANCES

# Renovating Hearts

## CAROL SCHOENIG

 Year of the Book
135 Glen Avenue
Glen Rock, PA 17327

ISBN: 978-1-64649-474-3 (paperback)
ISBN: 978-1-64649-475-0

Cover design GetCovers.com

Previously released as *The Caretaker,* Black Velvet Seductions Publishing.



All characters in this book are completely fictional. They exist only in the imagination of the author. Any similarity to any actual person or persons, living or dead, is completely coincidental.

# Chapter One

"Mom, you can't do this."

Phae sucked in a deep breath and counted to ten. "Kera, I am your mother. I am sixty-four years old. I can do whatever I want. I appreciate your concern, but I'm going whether you like it or not."

Pinching her bottom lip, Kera said, "I think you should see a doctor, Mom. I don't believe that you're being rational."

Phae glared at her daughter. She didn't know if she wanted to laugh, cry or be angry. She could feel a knot forming in her stomach as indignation jolted through her body. "What are you insinuating, Kera; that I can't make decisions for myself?" Phae could feel her face getting warm as her temper flared. "I can assure you I have been making decisions for this family since before you were born. Always putting everyone else's needs and wants first."

Phae took a deep breath. She looked across the room to where Kera stood with her palm over her mouth and her eyes shimmering with tears. For an instant, Phae saw a little twelve-year-old girl who needed her mother's understanding, not the thirty-eight-year-old teacher and mother of three that Kera had become.

*I'm handling this poorly*, she thought. *I don't want to argue with my daughter.*

She walked over to Kera and wrapped an arm around her.

"I'm sorry, Mom. I didn't mean for it to sound like I think you're incompetent."

Leading Kera over to the bed, Phae pushed aside her packing. "Sit, Kera. Maybe I can help you understand."

Phae began to pace and wring her hands, contemplating how to explain her decision without sounding as if she regretted her life.

"I didn't finish college. I worked and supported my parents and siblings, adding to the family coffers. When I met your dad, I was taking a few night courses on architecture. I dreamed of becoming an architect and designing fabulous buildings. I dreamed of going to Europe to see the ancient ruins and the architecture in Italy, Greece, and Spain."

Phae expelled a whoosh of breath. "Your father swept me off my feet at nineteen. We got married, and I left my parents' house and moved in with your father. I was blessed with two beautiful children. Your brother was a honeymoon baby, and you came along two years later. Your dad didn't want me to work. He believed he was the breadwinner, and we would get by on what he brought home. Life pulled me along, and I went wherever anyone needed me to be. I was happy with my life. I took care of you kids and took care of my parents and your dad's parents when they got old until they passed on.

"Kera, I don't regret my life. I loved your father; I love being a mom and grandmother, but at this stage of my life, I need an adventure. I want an adventure. I want to see a little of the world before I die. I had hoped when your father retired he might be more open to traveling. He died before we even had a chance to discuss it."

With pleading eyes, she implored Kera to understand. "I'm not waiting for someday anymore. My someday is here. I want to take advantage of this opportunity to live in Mallorca; to see the things I've always wanted to see. I want to be on my own and not have to worry about pleasing anyone but myself. I know you are concerned for me. Tell me what you are afraid of..."

"I'm worried about if you get sick or have a heart attack, or get mugged."

Phae shrugged. "Even if I didn't go, those are all possibilities." Phae walked over to the dresser. She picked up her cell phone and two boxes. "I got a new cell phone number that permits me to call or text internationally. As a going away gift, I bought you and your brother each one."

"What if you decide not to come back?"

Phae looked over the top of her glasses and smiled. "Really? This is my home. My family is here—you, your brother and my wonderful grandchildren. Besides, I'm looking forward to you all coming for a visit."

Kera cocked her head to one side and responded with, "Mom, what am I supposed to do for nine months while you are away?"

"Live your life, honey. That is what I am going to be doing." Kera rose and hugged her. "I'll miss you. And I'll still worry. Send lots of pictures, okay?"

Phae stroked her daughter's cheek, pushing hair away from her fair face. "I'll miss you too. Now help me finish packing."

## Chapter Two

$\mathcal{P}$hae had been in Spain for three days. She had spent the first two scrubbing the kitchen and bathrooms. Today she was going to reward herself by going outside to tackle the gardens. The wisteria and climbing David Austin roses were in need of pruning. The wisteria was a mass of tangled stems. The roses were blooming, but not as full as they should be. The dead flowers needed to come off. The branches of both the wisteria and roses needed to be shaped.

Opening the garden shed she found a six-foot ladder. Carefully, she opened it and placed it near the arbor. Grabbing the shears and a pair of gloves, she began pruning. She started at the bottom and worked her way up. Lost in her thoughts, she hummed and pruned. She climbed up to the next step of the ladder and held on to the arbor with one hand, stretching to reach the last straggling branch.

***

Finn rounded the corner of the drive. Movement near the top of the arbor startled him. He looked again. A large brimmed green hat bobbed and swung. His heart pounded in his chest and a knot formed in his stomach at the sight of the woman on the arbor. *If she falls, she will go tumbling down the rugged hillside.* The thought of the injuries she might sustain had his heart racing.

He got out of the car and sprinted to the arbor. As he approached, he saw the ladder begin to wobble. The ladder crashed to the ground and left the woman clinging to the arbor with both arms, her feet flailing.

Phae's hat had slipped over her eyes, and she couldn't see a thing. As she dangled midair she heard her daughter's voice warning her to be safe. If she let go she would tumble down the hill, and who knows how badly she would be hurt. She would dread telling Kera about this predicament when she came home. The thought of falling had a certain appeal, if it meant she'd avoid Kera's condemnation. Suddenly she felt an arm at her back and under her knees.

"Let go. I've got you," said a deep, authoritative voice.

Strong arms were holding her. Trembling, she turned from the arbor and pushed the hat up so she could see who had rescued her. Wisps of hair still covered her eyes. When she blew them away, she saw a square-jawed man. His steel-gray eyes peered down at her and his grip tightened, his expression stern as his frown deepened in confusion. "Who the hell are you?"

She glared at him. "Put me down. I belong here. I'm the caretaker. Who are you? You're trespassing on private property."

"I highly doubt you are the caretaker. I'm the owner, and I had specific requests of the agency."

Phae could feel the heat rising to her face. She felt at a disadvantage while he held her in his arms. "Could you please put me down?" she asked, biting her lower lip.

Gently, he lowered her to the ground. Phae was still a little shaken, and wobbled when he released her. He grabbed her elbow to steady her. Mortified that she had accused him of trespassing on his own property, she cleared her throat. "I'm not sure what you expected. I was told you wanted a grandmother to care for your home and daughter. I am a grandmother."

She lowered her eyes. "Please forgive me for accusing you of trespassing. I didn't know who you were, and you scared me."

He let go of her elbow. "Sit," he said.

Her eyes grew wide. She squared her shoulders and jutted her head up to look him in the eyes. "Did you command me to sit, as though I were a dog?"

***

It had been a long time since anyone had challenged his words or actions. For a petite woman, she was feisty. He liked that; it shot a flicker of life through his heart. He hadn't felt like that in a while.

He motioned for her to sit. "Let me introduce myself. Finn Callahan. Perhaps we should start over." Finn observed the look of panic cross her face. "I promise I won't bite."

Her eyes darted from the bench to his face. To put her at ease he said, "I'm sorry. I didn't mean for it to sound like a command. I'll sit as well." Finn eased his tall frame onto the bench. "You nearly gave me a heart attack, dangling from the arbor."

She removed her hat and gave him a little smile. "I don't know what I was thinking taking such a chance. It was rather scary, wasn't it?"

"So, you're the caretaker?" Finn didn't usually engage in small talk, but this woman had scared him into being concerned for her safety. He gave her a sideways glance. "I have no reservations that you will protect my property the way you stood your ground. But who is going to be watching over you?"

When she looked at him with those hazel eyes he thought his heart did a flip. "What made you want to leave your home and come to Spain?" Finn asked.

Phae let out a soft sigh. "I watched a documentary on Mallorca and the lemon and lime groves. The beauty I saw in the country, and the people, captured my heart; and it has been a dream of mine." She giggled. "It may sound crazy, but I rented out my house and put my things in storage. That is how much I wanted to come to Spain."

His breath caught in his throat. He had a profound need to know more. "What did your children say about this?"

She looked up to the heavens. "I had to remind them that I'm an adult. I'm getting on in years and this is on my bucket list." She laughed.

Finn didn't know if he wanted to laugh or frown so he smiled. He couldn't help but wonder what else was on that bucket list.

He was fascinated by her and listened to her animated story. He saw several strands of gray in her auburn hair as it caught the afternoon sunlight when she turned her head to look at him. A scattering of freckles danced across her high cheekbones, drawing his gaze to an oval-shaped face with only a few wrinkles near her eye— hazel eyes that were expressive and held gold flecks when she was excited.

Renting her home and storing her possessions had taken a lot of courage and confidence. He liked that he didn't feel as if he had to walk on eggshells around her.

"Where is home?"

She inhaled deeply and released her breath. "I'm from Glendale, Wisconsin. I have two children and four grandchildren who range from two to ten years of age. I was married for twenty-seven years before my husband became ill and left us."

Finn noticed her voice drop and the smile leave her face. He was familiar with that kind of pain.

"You said something about an adventure earlier," he asked, hoping to see the warmth light her face again.

She put her hands over her face, clearly embarrassed by what she'd said earlier. "It was foolish babble," she said, as she placed her hands back in her lap.

The adventure statement had intrigued him. He wanted to hear more. "I would be disappointed if you didn't tell me. I used to be adventurous." He gave her a quick wink and an enticing smile.

She gave him that mysterious smile again. "I want this job. When I was a young girl, I dreamt of becoming an architect and traveling abroad to see the world's great buildings. Instead, my husband came into my life, and it went in a different direction." She sighed. "I never had the opportunity. I decided I would take this job so I could experience another part of the world." Her eyes took on a dreamy quality. "Encounter other cultures."

Finn liked visiting other countries as well, but his wife hadn't wanted to leave her homeland. Over the years, he'd been married, his travel changed to trips back and forth from the United States for work to Spain to be with his family.

"Then you must be sure you take time to explore Mallorca while you are here. It is the pleasure island of Spain. I would recommend you drive up to the Tramuntana Mountains. They wrap around the most inspiring hill towns, fishing villages and quiet beaches. It is said that one does not need to root for lotus fruit because the scenery works its own spell." There was silence as he remembered his experience.

His eyes returned to her face. He found her to be charming and entertaining.

Just what his daughter needed.

Phae tilted her head and looked at him. "I'm curious. Why do you want a grandmother to take care of your daughter?"

Finn walked over and picked up the ladder. "My daughter is twenty. She will be returning here for the summer. I want someone who can make her cookies and spoil her with attention."

He rubbed his toe in the dirt thinking about the last summer they'd spent here.

He felt a stab of familiar pain in his chest. "She has not been here since her mother died when she was eight, and I am not sure how she will react."

"Don't you think it might be better if you were here?" Her eyes followed as he continued to stir the dirt with his toe. Phae fanned herself with her hat.

Finn noticed her face and arms were getting red. "We had better get you out of the sun before you turn into a lobster."

"I was thinking the same thing. I don't know about you, but I'm thirsty. I made fresh lemonade from the lemon trees in the back."

# Chapter Three

" Lemonade sounds fantastic." Finn stood to go into the house and waited for Phae to rise.

As she stood up, she swayed a little. Finn offered his hand. She hesitated, but finally took it. This was the second time he had touched her, and the second time he'd felt like he was standing on a live wire. Disappointment filled him when she released his hand.

They entered the yellow and white kitchen. As he stood in the dimly lit room, sadness swept over him. While Phae got glasses and poured lemonade, Finn looked around the kitchen.

He had not been in the house for ten years. Memories of coming home to find his wife in the kitchen, humming, filled him with sorrow. He could almost feel his little girl running and jumping into his arms, *"Daddy, Daddy!"* she'd squeal. Now the kitchen just looked old, dark and out of date. It felt empty.

The scent of pine teased his nostrils and brought him back to reality. Angelina was gone, and his daughter, Izzy, was grown now. She'd be returning to connect with her past in a few days. By the time Izzy arrived, he'd be back in the United States, lost in his grueling schedule.

Phae handed him the lemonade and waited. He raised the glass to his lips and took a large gulp. "Aghhh."

He squeezed his eyes shut and sucked in his cheeks. It was the worst lemonade he'd ever tasted. It had shocked him out of his reverie.

"Oh my gosh," Phae stammered. "I'm sorry. I forgot that I ran out of sugar this morning."

He wondered what she was up to as she ran from the kitchen. She returned with several packets. "Here, I found these in my purse."

She took his glass. Her hands shook as she stirred in the sugar. He moved closer to her. He wanted to ease her nervousness to let her know he wasn't angry about the lemonade… though it had been awful.

He longed to touch her, but he couldn't risk scaring her away. She was the right person to watch over Isabella. He didn't want to muddy things with a flirtation or worse, an affair, especially one that would end up being a long-distance relationship. Besides, she would be gone in six months. Anything between them would be more like two ships passing in the night than a lasting relationship. He also had a strict rule about getting involved with his employees, and she was an employee.

He saw the mirth lingering in her eyes. She looked up at him tentatively as she handed him the glass. There was no more than six inches between them. Her clean, sweet scent drifted to his nose, reminding him of sunshine and honeysuckle. He gazed into her eyes and took the glass. He didn't want to be, but he was drawn to her.

She stepped back, putting distance between them as if she felt it too. "Are you okay now? I am so sorry about the lemonade." She moved to the kitchen table and took a seat.

*Shrewd move putting the table between us*, he thought. "We were talking about your daughter's return."

He took a seat opposite her. He twirled the remains of the lemonade.

She rested her elbows on the table, clasped her hands and dropped her chin on her hands. "You're not sure how she will react when she comes here. Don't you think it would be better if you were here?"

He put the empty glass down and squeezed the bridge of his nose. He grappled with telling her what had happened between him and Izzy in the aftermath of his wife's death. She was a mother with two grown children. She'd stuck by her children, raising them alone when her husband had died. Phae had been through the teenage and early adult years with her children; maybe she could offer him some advice. "We don't have a relationship. It's my fault, and I don't know how to fix it."

She lowered her elbows and leaned further into the table with her fingers touching to form a steeple. He held his breath waiting for her to condemn him.

Instead, she said, "Tell me what happened."

He couldn't bear to look at her. "Isabella was eight years old when her mother died. We left two days after the funeral. We haven't been back since."

He could feel his heart tightening as he talked. "We returned to the United States, and I sent her to a private school. At first, we talked a couple of times a month. But I didn't know how to deal with a sobbing child. At holidays, rather than have her come home, I sent her to my brother's house in Iowa." He gulped down the lump in his throat, remembering how Izzy had begged him to come back.

He played with the glass in his hand. He kept his eyes on the table, studying the rings of condensation the glass left. "I wasn't capable of caring for a grief-stricken child. I was struggling with my own pain. I threw myself into my work during the day. At night, I'd drown my sorrows in alcohol. I didn't want her to see me like that." He sat there and remembered how, at first, she would cry and ask when he was coming to get her. After a while, she'd stopped asking, and he'd ceased making excuses; but it hadn't gotten easier.

His heart shattered thinking about what he had done. How self-centered he had been. As time went on, he'd improved. His work kept him busy, and the company grew. He managed to get himself off the bottle. He tried dating a few times, but by then the gulf between him and Izzy had grown. He shook his head. "I was a terrible father. I abandoned my daughter when she needed me most."

Finn ventured a glance at Phae. He wanted to see her reaction, though he dreaded seeing his self-condemnation mirrored in her eyes. Instead, she just sat there, listening. He stood up and paced back and forth between the table and the stove. He found moving around gave him the courage to continue. "We didn't talk very much after that, mostly messages on an answering machine, or e-mails. We seemed to miss each other's calls. We would see each other maybe four times a year. We didn't have much to talk about, because by then we had become strangers."

Phae looked at him. Surprise and disappointment shone in her eyes.

"A month ago, Izzy sent me an e-mail. She told me she wanted to come to Spain for the summer. She wanted to see the house where she was born and where she'd spent the first eight years of her life. I told her I had to think about it." He rubbed his right temple. "After how I treated her, I couldn't deny her this request. Besides, the villa is sitting here rotting away. A decision needs to be made about the property."

His body was wound tight, and he was perspiring. He held his breath and waited for her to say something. He could imagine her taking him to task for the way he'd abandoned Izzy, but it wouldn't be anything that he hadn't already done himself. He just hoped that after hearing all this, she would stay for Isabella's sake.

Phae cleared her throat. He held his breath. "Finn, people grieve in different ways. Some people do as you did—throw themselves into work and drinking. I threw myself into a flurry of activities. I didn't have the financial luxury to send my children away. I can't say if I would or wouldn't have."

Finn was surprised. He had never thought about what he would have done if he hadn't had the money to send Izzy away.

"I believe you did the best you could, given the circumstances. I also believe sometimes it is more difficult for a man to take over the role of mother and father than it is for a woman."

She came to him and put her hand on his shoulder. "I don't know whom I feel sadder for, you or Isabella. You may have lost your wife, but Isabella lost her mother due to illness, and then she lost her father, and she didn't know why."

Finn looked at Phae and saw tears shimmering in her eyes. He felt so ashamed; not just for what he'd done to Izzy, but for the feelings that stirred inside him. He longed to have someone touch him with gentleness and caring. But this woman was his employee.

"I'm not sure I understand what you want me to say to you. I only know that it is never too late to tell children I'm sorry, or I love you."

When she walked away from him, a shiver ran through his body.

"My suggestion is that you call her. Tell her you're sorry and that you love her. Then I think you need to find time to be here when she arrives."

Her words rang in his ears. She had a way of getting him to think about different perspectives, about what was the right thing to do. She hadn't judged or found him a selfish jerk; she'd listened, acknowledging both his and Izzy's grief, then she'd pointed out a way forward.

Phae picked up the glasses and rinsed them out. She patted him on the shoulder and left the room.

In a couple of minutes, she returned with an overnight bag. "I'm heading down to the hotel. Let the agency know when it is okay for me to return."

He wanted to beg her not to leave. He didn't want to be alone in this house with ghosts and painful memories. He was also afraid that, if she stayed, he would regret it. He couldn't deny that he found her attractive. Finn had the sense that, if they'd met under other circumstances, they would have become friends, maybe lovers. He had to be honest with himself; he wanted more from her than sympathy. He'd not felt connected to anyone since his wife had died. With Phae, there'd been a connection, and he found himself reluctant to let it go.

"Let me take that. I'll walk you out to your car." They walked in silence. He tossed her bag into the backseat and opened the front door for her.

They stood there for a moment as the setting sun cast a warm glow across the valley. He reached out and stroked her face. He enjoyed the softness of her cheek. He lifted her chin and gently pressed his lips to hers.

He felt her hand slide between them, separating them and pushing him away. "Finn, I didn't come to Spain to look for romance. I'm your employee. I don't want any complications."

Her rejection hurt, but it brought him to his senses. She was right. She was his employee, and he should have kept things strictly professional. He hadn't intended to make things awkward for her. He wanted her to stay and take care of Izzy.

He watched Phae drive away until the car was no longer visible. When it disappeared from sight, he felt more alone than ever.

# Chapter Four

Phae forced herself not to look in the rear view mirror. She touched her lips expecting to feel them singed.

That kiss may have been gentle, but it had ignited something deep within her. If she hadn't broken the kiss when she had, she would have given in to it. It had made her feel cared for and beautiful—two things she hadn't felt in a long time.

Finn had a commanding, distinguished appearance that drew her eyes. He towered over her, making her feel petite, which was odd for a woman of her height. She shivered, remembering how secure she felt in his arms when he'd caught her dangling off the arbor.

She had wanted to touch him, but she'd been afraid. She'd avoided dating and relationships with men for so long she now just accepted her single status. Initially, she had been too tired and emotionally exhausted to think about dating. Later, she had been embarrassed that she'd not kept up with styles and hadn't tried to look feminine. She'd lived an androgynous existence, going about her business, working, raising her kids, keeping up the house.

She'd accepted life without a man. She was content to be independent. It felt strange to find herself attracted to this man after so many years of being on her own.

When he'd looked at her, her body temperature had risen. His touch was gentle when he'd stroked her cheek. The kiss itself had been delicious. She couldn't recall the last time she'd been kissed like that.

She tightened her hands on the steering wheel. She hoped she still had a job come tomorrow. After all, she'd rejected the boss.

She wondered if he'd been expecting a mistress as well as a caretaker. Then she shook her head. That wasn't Finn. She may not have known him well, but she knew he had loved his wife deeply. Though he didn't have a stellar relationship with his daughter, he had taken responsibility for his failings as a father. It was clear he loved his daughter.

Phae turned the radio on to rid herself of those fanciful notions. She sang along to "Will You Love Me Tomorrow," but the song just made her sad, and she turned the radio off. She hadn't thought of love or romance in a long time. If she got involved with Finn, what would they have? She wasn't a one- night stand kind of woman. She'd want to know he would love her.

She was torn. She missed her husband's ability to repair things at home, even if it was grudgingly. It had taken her a while to get used to the fact that she was alone in the house at night. She had admired his work ethic. He may not have showered her with gifts and jewelry, but he did provide a nice roof over their heads, food and cars. They hadn't had any financial worries until he got sick. She didn't miss the arguments over silly things, like how many miles she put on the car, or him waking her up in the middle of the night to yell about something she hadn't put away. She was grateful for the time they'd had together, but about four years after his death she'd suddenly realized she had her independence back. She didn't have to worry about how many miles she put on the car. She found peace in knowing she didn't have to walk on eggshells, or have to ask anyone else's permission about what color to paint the house, or what flowers to plant. She didn't have to explain her comings and goings. She had been tired of letting go of her wants and desires for her husband, and of being manipulated to do what her family wanted.

She'd thought about their marriage and realized they may not have been able to stand the test of time. They'd wanted different things. It had been okay during the years they were raising a family, when their focus had been on building a home, but when the kids had grown up and moved out into the world on their own, would they still have been compatible, or would the differences have separated them?

Even if Finn did eventually want more than a one-night stand, would she? She wasn't dependent on anyone for money. She was able to pursue the hobbies she enjoyed. Up until now, she'd been having too much fun to want a relationship.

Biting her lip, Phae remembered her friend Jenna insisting, in her brash way, that most widowed men wanted someone to cook for them and have sex with them.

Nope, Phae was not interested in dating. Her freedom meant more to her than cooking and a man in her bed.

When Phae arrived at the hotel, her heart swelled in excitement at the splendor before her.

The black and white marble that spanned the lobby flickered in the soft yellow glow cast by gold chandeliers. The scattering of Vimercati furniture, which she recognized from a magazine article, made her feel like she had stepped into a different time. Bowls of fresh lemons and flowers were placed on tables, and their fragrance infused the lobby.

Phae glanced at her watch; it was six o'clock. She decided to check in and grab a light supper, so she could walk around the city before it got dark. She would do some window shopping.

She walked down the narrow stone sidewalks. In one store window, her eye was drawn to a mannequin dressed in a light cotton nightie trimmed with lace along the straps and bodice. Little rosebuds adorned the fabric. It looked feminine. Her night attire was pajamas or sweat pants and tee shirts. She hadn't worn anything feminine to bed since before her husband got sick.

Her heart fluttered at the memory of the sensual feeling of wearing clothes that would arouse a man—something that was lost on George. A memory flashed of him telling her, *"What are you made up for? We're taking care of a bodily need, not seduction."* It had made her feel cheap and uncared for.

Finn had made her feel sexy, and she wanted that feeling again. In the privacy of her room, she could wear the charming garment and revel in her femininity. With a sensual mindset, she almost floated into the boutique. Gently she let the fabric fall through her fingers, imagining the way it would brush over her body. She closed her eyes and could almost feel fingertips sliding the straps off her shoulders.

"May I help you?"

Phae jumped, and her heart pounded as she opened her eyes to see a gray-haired, petite woman looking at her.

"I didn't mean to startle you."

"That's okay. I was just lost in memories."

The woman smiled and said, "We women are like that; even at my age I yearn to see the light of love in my husband's eyes. But alas, he is in a better place. Are you looking for something to spark your husband's eyes?"

Phae lowered her head and wrung her hands. "No, he is gone. I just want to feel attractive."

The saleswoman patted her arm. "I understand; sometimes it is what we wear underneath that makes us feel like a woman."

Phae smiled. She bought the nightgown and several sets of matching bras and panties.

# Chapter Five

She returned to the hotel with her new lingerie, and drew water for a long leisurely bath, scenting it with soap shaped like rose petals. She lit a few candles on the vanity and then sank down into the luxurious tub, put her head back and closed her eyes.

When she dozed off, a dream wove through her subconscious. She'd visited another country. She laughed at something as someone snapped her picture. Phae heard the sound of church bells, but they were harsh, not melodic. She opened her eyes and realized the church bells she'd dreamed were actually the telephone ringing.

Quickly she wrapped one of the giant bath towels around her and scurried across the room. She was a little disoriented and breathless as she picked up the phone and said, "Hello."

"Is this Phae Carson?" the voice asked.

"Yes," she said in a husky voice.

"I apologize if I woke you. This is Finn Callahan."

She pulled the towel tighter and took a deep breath; her entire body tense as queasiness filled her stomach.

Had he called to fire her? "Is something wrong?"

She could hear Finn taking a deep breath. Her queasiness increased. "I called earlier, but the desk informed me that you were not in. Where were you?"

The slightly petulant tone of his voice struck a chord in her, reminding her of the way George had kept her under his thumb, always wanting to know where she was, what she did.

She clenched her fist and rolled her eyes upward. "Excuse me? I don't believe that is any of your business." No sooner had the words passed her lips than she thought about her job. Aghast at what she'd said, she covered her mouth, berating herself.

Before she could say anything, he apologized, "I'm sorry. You are correct; it isn't any of my business. I called to see if you had arrived safely, and to ask if we could have lunch tomorrow."

She sat on the edge of the bed, looking at the floor and shaking her foot, her fingers rubbing her forehead. The seeds of panic invaded her body, and her breathing became constricted. It felt as though she was suffocating.

She opened her eyes and shook her head. She didn't want to become embroiled in a relationship. She wanted to be her own person for a while, to do what she wanted. She had been everyone's doormat for far too long. It was her turn.

She cleared her throat and shivered. "Yes, I'll have lunch with you."

"Good. I'll pick you up around noon. Good night."

Phae disconnected the call. She wrapped her arms around herself and her thoughts scattered. When she was near Finn, she yearned to feel desirable. She couldn't breathe, and her hands itched to touch him. She feared he could see the lust in her eyes.

Phae inhaled deeply and told herself to get a grip; she was a master at burying her real feelings. She would hide her fantasies of Finn and enjoy her time in Spain.

***

Finn hung up the phone reluctantly. He liked talking to Phae; her soft and breathless voice was soothing.

He lay down on the sofa, hoping she would accept this new project.

It was time for him to move on and put his wife's ghost to rest once and for all. He needed to mend his relationship with his daughter. He hadn't planned on ever returning to Spain, but now that he was here, he didn't want to leave.

As soon as he drifted off to sleep, he dreamt of his wife. She haunted him periodically, and it was always the same dream. She was lying in their bed, hardly able to breathe and in tremendous pain. She clutched his hand, *"Be happy,"* she'd beg.

He'd console her by saying, *"I'm happy here with you."* Then she would vanish.

Opening his eyes, he looked up at the ceiling, wondering if he could find happiness again.

# Chapter Six

$\mathcal{F}$inn arrived at the hotel at 12:15 P.M. He was leaning on the passenger side of the car, waiting for Phae to come out of the hotel. Five minutes later he saw her step out, a wide brimmed hat on her head, sunglasses dangling from her hand, which she lifted to shield against the sun. He walked toward her. His instinct was to kiss her on the cheek. Instead, he put his hands in his pockets.

"Good afternoon. It's a beautiful day today," he greeted her.

"Yes, yes, it is."

"My car is this way."

As they strolled to the vehicle, he glanced at her sideways. He noticed she was a little pale, and her body seemed rigid. She clung to her purse as though it were a lifeline. She looked over at him, and he looked away. He didn't want her to see desire on his face. *This is not going to be an easy sale*, he thought.

He helped her into the car. When he got behind the wheel, he said, "My favorite restaurant is up in the hills. They serve authentic Spanish dishes made with what is harvested here on Mallorca. I remember that you said you wanted to see the country, so I thought it would give us the opportunity to kill two birds with one stone."

He glanced over to see her reaction. She sat stiffly, with her hands folded on her lap. He frowned, unsure of what to say to put her at ease. "Phae, have I done something to offend you? You look like you're going to the gallows. Are you miffed about the kiss?"

"It's not you, Finn. It's me."

"I don't understand." He shook his head in confusion. "Do you want to go back to the hotel? I just wanted to do something nice for you."

He watched as several emotions skittered across her face. Sadness and dissonance were the most prominent, as though she was reluctant to voice her thoughts. "You can tell me what's upsetting you. I won't fire you, if that's what's worrying you."

"That's just it. I'm not used to people wanting to please me. I'm usually the one seeing to everyone else's needs."

She avoided his gaze, and he sensed she was holding something back. It seemed like the novelty of it should let her enjoy the outing, but her expression was so somber it made him want to reach out and physically wipe the sadness away. "That's even more reason for you to just sit back and enjoy the scenery," he said instead.

She shrugged. "Perhaps you're right. I do appreciate the gesture, it's just… a new experience for me." She closed her eyes and took a calming breath while continuing to rub her hands. He couldn't help thinking that if she could sprout wings she'd take off.

Finn pulled over and stopped the car. He turned sideways to face her, one arm over the back of her seat. "Phae, I honestly am just interested in sharing some of the sights of Mallorca with you. No strings, no ulterior motives. It's been a long time since I've had a chance to explore, and Mallorca should be seen with someone and not alone." He watched as she lowered her head. "My ulterior motive is spending time getting to know you and hopefully sharing a beautiful day and an excellent meal."

She winced and swallowed a gulp. "You have a very expressive face, and I like seeing it light up when you talk about having adventures and seeing new things."

She lifted her head to look at him, and he thought he saw some signs of acquiescence.

"As much as I enjoyed the kiss, I promise I won't kiss you again, unless you want me to."

He watched, captivated by the rise and fall of her chest as she stroked her neck with her fingertips, as if she were warring with herself. He wondered what was wreaking havoc on her mind as her beautiful hazel eyes clouded over.

His heart tightened as she twirled her bracelet, looking anywhere but at him.

He remained silent, letting her have time to consider his words. "Phae?"

She was biting her thumbnail. "I'm just… It is a very thoughtful gesture, and you whetted my appetite for both the scenery and the restaurant."

"Do I take that as a 'yes'?"

Finn watched as she nodded in agreement. Some of the anxiety that had filled her face eased, and some of the excitement that had lit her face the day before, when she'd talked about the things she wanted to see, took up residence.

"Would you like the top down? It blows the cobwebs out of one's mind."

When she agreed, her eyes held an inner glow. He pushed a button, and the whirr of the motor collapsing the top prevented further discussion. Finn shifted gears and eased the car back onto the roadway.

Phae tried to hold her hat down. Finally, she let out a jingle of laughter and removed the hat. The wind whipping her hair all about, she glanced over at Finn. "This is delightful, I feel like I'm twenty years old again."

Finn laughed as he shifted gear to continue the climb to the top of the mountain. As they made their way up, Finn pointed to the Mediterranean Sea and Barcelona, explaining that Mallorca was a hundred and twenty miles south of Barcelona, and was the largest island of the Balearic chain.

Finn was disappointed when she put on her sunglasses, which hid her eyes from him. He wanted to see the joy in her expression as she took in the sights, sounds, and smells of the island. Warmth radiated through his body each time he heard her intake of air and heard her whisper, "It's so beautiful."

When they arrived at the restaurant, Finn's heart beat a little faster at the elegantly restored manor inn before him. Its stone pillars and numerous varieties of flowers accentuated the tranquility of the area. He liked it here; it was peaceful. He'd picked it because of its architecture and its gardens, hoping Phae would enjoy it as much as he did. He didn't take his eyes off of her as he turned off the engine. He wanted the pleasure of seeing wonder and happiness on her face.

Phae put her hand to her throat, giving Finn a quick glance.

Without saying a word, he got out of the car and went to open the door for her, offering her his hand. When she took it, he felt the same zap of energy he'd felt when they'd touched and when they'd kissed the night before.

He heard her little gasps of air and delighted sighs as they moved toward the restaurant's entrance. Phae had removed her sunglasses, and the look of pleasure in her eyes mirrored the desire in his heart. She hugged his arm, and he was delighted that she had drawn close to him. She released his arm to walk up the three steps into the lobby, and he immediately missed her warmth.

As they stepped into the lobby, he looked up at the cedar ceiling adorned with intricate carvings. He glanced at Phae and knew that she saw it too.

"Isn't it beautiful? They uncovered the wooden ceiling during the renovations," he told her.

The *maître d'* approached. "*Señor* Callahan! It has been a long time since you have been here. Ahh. You bring with you a *bella señorita*. The man bowed in front of Phae. "Welcome to Grand Hotel Sonnet."

"Pedro, it is good to see you," Finn said and embraced the man.

"When I saw your name on the reservation list, I saved you the best table. This way, please."

As they walked through the beautiful lobby, sunlight bounced off metal swords that hung on the wall. Every time he saw them, they reminded Finn of Zorro—a man hiding behind a mask.

Finn turned to look at Phae. She had stopped to gaze at a mural. Its exquisite detail and vibrant colors captured Mallorca in the seventeenth century.

Breathless, she whispered, "It's... *muy hermoso!*"

They were led to a patio on the other side of the lobby. A table covered with white linen rested up against a stone half wall. Bougainvillea hung from the trellised roof, and potted plants and flowers of varying sizes and shapes were scattered about. A spectacular view of the sea and smaller islands was before them. Finn smiled as Phae's eyes grew wide with excitement.

The *maître d'* pulled her chair out and seated her, and then excused himself.

As Finn took his place, he caught a whiff of her lavender shampoo. He liked the scent.

Finn looked at Phae and said, "I hope this made you happy that you accepted my invitation to lunch."

"It's so much to take in. Between the beauty and the history, it's overwhelming. Thank you."

Finn motioned for the sommelier to come to their table, and requested a bottle of Heredad De Penalosa.

Finn was quiet as he observed Phae. Her eyes had a dreamy look as she looked out toward the sea, her head resting on her hands. "Penny for your thoughts."

She dropped her hands and looked at him with sultry eyes. "I was thinking how beautiful it all is. How peaceful."

"You feel it too." He smiled and poured them each a glass of wine. "What should we toast to?"

"Anything you want."

Lifting his glass Finn said, "To new adventures and friendships." They clinked glasses and sipped their wine.

"Do you have any preferences... beef, fish, chicken?"

"I like all three. I like vegetables and salads too." She shrugged her right shoulder. "I'm not a picky eater."

He watched as she tilted her head and tapped her chin. "This is my first experience eating near the sea. I think it would be sacrilegious to not eat fish when you are near a seaport."

Finn couldn't help smiling. That was his sentiment as well.

"Would you like to preview the menu or would you like me to order for both of us?"

She smiled at Finn, and he thought his heart flip-flopped in his chest. "Please order for both of us. I would rather enjoy the view than spend time studying the menu."

He ordered their meal of baked monkfish paired with a citrus risotto, and almond cake for dessert.

As he placed their order, he glanced at her to gauge her reaction. "I hope you like what I ordered."

"I'm sure I will. What can you tell me about this place?" she asked, leaning forward.

They chatted about the scenery and cuisine as they ate their lunch.

When they'd finished, Finn excused himself. When he returned, he was carrying her sketchbook.

"I found this on the kitchen counter. You have some excellent ideas on renovations for my house."

She raised her fingers over her mouth, clearly embarrassed. He found it charming. "I'm sorry Finn. I was just imagining what it would look like with a makeover."

He covered her hand with his. "Nothing to be sorry about. I know you'd said you had hopes of becoming an architect. What courses have you taken?"

She looked at him with questioning eyes. "I studied Design I through Design III and Structures, New Worlds and Old, and Construction Management. What is this all about?"

"Your drawings made me realize that, if I wanted to sell the villa in the future, I would need to do some serious renovations. I thought that since you drew these up, maybe you would like to be a project manager and oversee the construction."

# Chapter Seven

Finn watched as Phae's mouth dropped open, and then her lips pressed together. She'd gone from excited to frowning in the space of a heartbeat. "What's wrong? Did I say something to upset you?"

She looked down at the floor and folded her napkin, placing it on the table.

Her words were halting as she said in a thick voice, "I'll have to decline for now."

Finn sat back to study her. "I don't understand. I thought this would make you happy."

Phae took a sip of her wine. Her mind was racing. What would his daughter think or say if she came home looking for a connection to her mother and to the memories of her early childhood, to find everything had changed with new paint and wall and floor coverings? Phae understood that desire to hold on to one's mother. She had lost her own when she was in her twenties.

She had let her guard down and had been enjoying herself and the beautiful surroundings. She didn't want to be suspicious, but why would he offer her such a fantastic opportunity, especially when he should be thinking of his daughter's happiness, not hers.

She couldn't accept this without knowing that Izzy would be on board with the renovation. It was Izzy's home, and she might have different ideas.

If Phae agreed to take this on it would also mean that they would be spending lots of time either on the phone or in person. If she said yes, she would be making a commitment of her time and energy for someone else, even if it fulfilled a dream of hers. It would definitely take away from the time she had available to explore Mallorca.

"I'd like to hear an explanation."

She sat there looking at him, feeling disappointment and sadness as she tried to make sense of her own feelings. "Finn, I couldn't possibly accept this now because it wouldn't be right. Your daughter is coming to Mallorca to see her childhood home. To see her roots, and remember her mother."

As Finn swirled the wine in his glass, Phae saw the same sadness and disappointment she felt mirrored in his eyes.

He folded his hands on the table and let out a sigh. "That was insensitive of me, and you are correct. I guess wanting to make you happy made me forget about my daughter's visit."

They sat gazing out at the sea, deep in their own thoughts.

"Finn, why do you want to make me happy? We've only known each other two days." She held her breath, waiting for his reply.

He smiled slightly. "Has it been only two days? I feel like we have known each other longer than that." He looked her straight in the eye. "I swear to you the only ulterior motive was to have an excuse to get to know you better. I would like to get my home renovated, and I do like to see you smile."

"It was a very thoughtful gesture, and I'd love to accept, but I'm going to make a suggestion and see what you think."

The hopeful look in his eyes gave Phae the courage to continue.

"Maybe wait until Isabella arrives, get a sense of what she is feeling toward both coming home and seeing you. If she would be eager for the renovations, perhaps it would be a way for the two of you to heal and bond together over the project. It might give you a way to reconnect."

Phae sipped her water to stall for time to digest her own thoughts and feelings, and to give Finn the opportunity to do the same.

She glanced up and caught him staring at her. "You… are brilliant."

"Really, you like the idea?" The tension eased from her body.

As they waited for dessert to arrive, they talked a little about her architecture studies. Finishing the last morsels of their almond cake, they agreed it was hard to leave. Finn motioned to the waiter for the check and said his goodbye to Pedro with a promise to return.

As they drove down the mountain, Finn didn't say anything, and it was making Phae crazy. She couldn't help but wonder if maybe he had changed his mind about the renovation.

His words drew Phae out of her reverie. "I know that we need to talk to Izzy first… or I should say, I need to speak with Izzy first, but in the meantime, could you complete the sketches?"

She looked up. His eyes were on the road, and, for an instant, she wanted to kiss him. Instead, she replied, "I would love to. Thank you."

They arrived at the hotel, and she turned to look at him. "Finn, I hope this will bring you and Izzy together."

"I think I need to make an appointment to see my daughter. If she won't have lunch with me then maybe we can at least talk on the phone." Tiny beads of sweat dotted his forehead, and he frowned. His fingers stroked her arm. "I'm leaving for the States early tomorrow morning. You are welcome to return to the villa, on one condition." She felt her heart racing, as he said, "You are not to climb any more ladders."

She smiled. "I understand."

He got out of the car and walked around to open the door for her. He walked beside her to the hotel entrance, hands in his pockets. His eyes met hers as he murmured, "Goodnight, Phae," his voice thick with emotion.

Her heart rate increased, and she swallowed. She was about ready to ask him to kiss her. Instead, she whispered, "Goodnight, Finn."

He turned to walk away.

Her thoughts spun through the events of the day. He had been so kind and generous with both his time and money. He may have promised not to kiss her again unless she asked, but she hadn't promised not to kiss him.

"Finn?" She moved in front of him and stood on her tiptoes to kiss him on the cheek. "Thank you for an enjoyable afternoon. Have a safe trip."

Then she turned and went into the hotel without looking back. *I'm going to miss him*, she thought, surprised at herself. How could she miss someone she'd only known for two days?

When Phae arrived at her suite, she felt restless. She changed into her nightwear and took a glass of wine out onto the veranda and sat looking at the blue-black sky, illuminated by a million stars and a full moon. She could hear the sea crashing up against the rocks and, in the distance, a ship's horn blasting.

Phae liked Finn, but she found it unsettling that he and his daughter were estranged. She offered up a prayer of thanks that she and her children had not drifted apart. Even if it meant she had lost part of herself. She would rather lose her own identity than lose her children.

# Chapter Eight

Phae awoke the next morning feeling rested and full of energy. She wanted to get back to the villa and tackle the rest of the cleaning before Isabella arrived. Not knowing when Finn's daughter might turn up, Phae wanted to be sure everything was done beforehand.

When she entered the villa, she thought perhaps Finn had changed his mind and was still there. The scent of his aftershave lingered in the air, tickling her nose and reminding her of the kiss she had given him the night before. She called out, but there was no answer.

She walked from room to room, her thoughts on how to keep the integrity of the design and history while adding warmth and a sense of peace and tranquility. The heavy drapes and dark, worn furniture were depressing.

She could picture sheer curtains draped over a decorative rod, the walls lightened with a pallet of tan, white, and pale aqua that would bring the beauty of the gardens indoors. It didn't matter, though; Izzy wanted to see her childhood home. Izzy was a grown woman; she had the right to change the rooms to fit her style and comfort.

Phae went upstairs, deposited her overnight bag, and changed into work clothes. She hadn't looked into any of the bedrooms yet because she'd felt awkward intruding into personal spaces. Still, she needed to get Isabella's room ready.

There were five closed doors. She tried the first one on the left and found it was locked. She thought that rather odd, but moved to the second, and slowly eased it open, noting the musty smell mixed with… she sniffed the air… dried roses.

Phae flipped on the light switch. Once her eyes adjusted to the light, she saw a twin bed with a faded pink canopy. Stuffed animals were thrown all about the room and a broken dollhouse sat in the corner as if a child had been interrupted mid temper tantrum and everything had been left exactly as it was.

She covered her lips with her fingers as she thought about Isabella. She remembered her own daughter's eight-year-old temper tantrums, how she'd sometimes wanted to rip her dollies' heads off. Phae wondered if Izzy had been angry because her mother had died or because her father was taking her away from her home.

Phae walked over to the window and pushed the heavy drapes aside. Coughing and sneezing from the dust, she quickly opened the window to get fresh air into the room. Next, she left to go downstairs and get cleaning supplies.

As she walked down the hall, she was curious about where Finn slept. Going from door to door peering into each room, she found that all of them were dark and held that old house smell. Not one of them looked as though it had been slept in recently. Perhaps his was the locked door.

She went downstairs and into the laundry room on the other side of the kitchen. As she passed the table, she saw a note addressed to her. She picked it up and read:

*My dear Phae,*

*I wanted to thank you for a delightful day yesterday. Words cannot express how grateful I am for your compassion and ability to bring me back the reality of what I must do for my daughter.*

*Please be careful while I am gone. I look forward to seeing you soon.*

*If you need anything, please don't hesitate to call me. My cell number is 319-474-0143.*

*Deep regards, Finn*

The note touched Phae, as it demonstrated that he had thought about her and was grateful rather than angry with her for rejecting his offer until he talked to Izzy. She held the note to her heart and closed her eyes just for a second. The more she got to know him, the more he seemed to be a kind and thoughtful man—one who had caused her latent sexuality to begin to thaw.

Phae gathered her cleaning supplies, went back upstairs, and proceeded to strip the bed linens. She took them downstairs and threw them into the washer. She picked up the dolls and stuffed animals and put them in a basket that she found.

She went about her business dusting and vacuuming, thoughts of Finn and Izzy claiming her mind. She glanced around the room, noting the worn areas of the dark carpet and imagining how painful it must have been for Finn to tell his daughter her mother was gone and that they were leaving their home.

Phae grew tired; she was not as young as she used to be. She vowed that tomorrow she would work on the walls and windows in Izzy's room. She wanted it to smell nice and to be clean and inviting… at least as inviting as the faded pink canopy and worn carpet allowed. She sat on the bed to gain enough energy to go downstairs. Her heart ached for both Finn and Izzy.

She understood Finn shutting off his emotions. She had done the same, but instead threw herself into a flurry of activity. What had driven Finn to ignore his daughter for so long, she wondered? How could he have not wanted his daughter with him?

# Chapter Nine

Isabella drove up the road in her rental car.

She craned her neck, looking for the first signs of her home, full of anticipation, imagining it as it had been ten years earlier. Her heart wrenched at the sight of overgrown plants and weeds in the garden. She remembered sitting under the arbor for what her mother had called their "girl talks." The arbor had been covered with purple flowers that hung like grapes. Red rose bushes scattered about had delivered a beautiful fragrance.

The house now had that abandoned look; moss grew on the outside walls of the villa and the windows appeared dark. She knew the feeling well… she had been abandoned after her mother's death. Only her heart wasn't covered with moss, it was covered with pain and sorrow.

She sat in the car and stared at the home where she had spent the first eight years of her life. She had come back because the memories of her mother and her early childhood were fading. Yet she was afraid to relive the pain and loss of her mother's death. If she was honest, she was trying to remember the happy family she'd once had. She draped her arms over the steering wheel and laid her head on her arms. Back then the house had been loved. There had been music and laughter. She and her parents had played hide-and-seek in the garden. She remembered her father laughing, scooping her up. When she'd been young, before her mother's death, she'd felt loved even adored by both her parents. It wasn't until her mother's death that her dad had grown distant and sent her away.

Until recently, anger consumed her. Now she was carrying a baby, and she felt the need to heal the rift between her and her father, to see if they could be a family again. She wanted to give her little one the loving family she'd once had. She wanted… no, she needed her father. It had taken her a while to realize part of her anger stemmed from wanting her dad to love her again.

She wanted the fun-loving father to be a grandfather to her child. She wanted to hear him laugh and see him toss a giggling grandson or granddaughter into the air. She didn't know what she'd do if he remained aloof and distant; she couldn't subject her child to that kind of person.

Izzy went into the villa and climbed the stairs, listening, as her eyes darted around looking for signs of an intruder, animal or human. She heard what sounded like a squeaky step and tiptoed to the door. Adrenaline pumped through her. The thought of seeing her dad caused her to stiffen her spine and inch the door open. She was still angry with him, yet she wanted him to hug her and make her feel better. She had a headache, and her stomach was churning. She felt scared and sad. Most of all she was worried that he may not love her anymore. Then she would be all alone in the world… except. She shook her head not wanting to think about it.

"Dad," Izzy called.

There was a crash and then the sound of a woman groaning. Her mind raced as she wondered who could be in there and what had caused the noise. She hesitated and considered calling the police, and then realized it would be ages before they got there. She closed her eyes and gulped, steadying herself before she made her move.

Izzy peeked into the room. A woman lay crumpled on the floor with a ladder on top of her. She wondered who this person was and what they were doing. The house was supposed to be empty. "Oh my God. What happened?" Izzy exclaimed.

Izzy knelt down and scanned the woman to see if she was bleeding anywhere. She guessed the woman might be in her late forties as she wore Capri jeans and a green tee shirt.

The woman opened her eyes and stared at the ceiling for a moment. Letting out a groan, she said, "You must be Isabella. I had hoped to get your room done before you arrived."

The last thing on her mind was her bedroom. "Are you hurt? What can I do to help?"

Izzy sat back, puzzled that this woman knew her name. She searched her memory trying to recall if her father had mentioned that someone would be here. "Who are you?"

Putting her right hand out to shake Izzy's, the woman said, "I'm Phae Carson. Your dad hired me as a caretaker to ready the house for your homecoming."

Izzy hesitated as she took Phae's hand. Her skin was warm and smooth, and Izzy saw that she had kind eyes that were searching her face, though for what she wasn't sure. "Let me help you up."

Once she got Phae righted and helped her to a chair, she allowed herself to look around the room.

Izzy walked to the bed and gently touched one of the bedposts. The basket of stuffed animals sat on the mattress, and she walked her fingers over each animal until she saw her pink elephant. She tilted her head to the side and felt a flutter in her heart. She pulled it out of the basket and whispered, "Well hello, Ms. Elly." Clutching the elephant, she walked to the window and peered out. The countryside was just as beautiful as she remembered.

In a soft, quiet voice Phae asked, "Do you want me to leave you alone?"

Izzy shook her head. Her movements were unhurried as she drifted back to the past, forgetting that Phae was sitting on the chair behind her.

Izzy's eyes traveled to the corner of the room where she saw her broken dollhouse. She stared at it as her father's words came back to her. *"Izzy, you remember how we talked about your Mom going to heaven?"* She saw herself nodding and him kneeling down in front of her. *"She has gone to heaven like we talked about."* She remembered screaming at him, *"No Daddy, no Daddy, I don't believe you."* He had hugged her, and she felt the tears on his cheek as their faces touched. He had held her while they both sobbed. When he'd tried to settle his large frame to sit on the floor, he accidentally kicked her dollhouse and broke it.

Izzy sucked in her lips and squeezed her eyes shut as the painful memory jabbed at her heart.

Somewhere in the distance, she heard a voice. "I can leave you with your thoughts." She opened her eyes to see Phae standing close and wringing her hands. As the woman closed the distance, Phae opened her arms and Izzy went into them.

Warm arms closed around her, and a gentle hand stroked her hair. Shhh… shhh," Phae soothed.

Izzy let the dam break, all the pain and hurt and anger frittered away as Phae held her close.

After a few minutes, she pulled herself together and moved out of Phae's embrace. "I..."

"You don't need to say anything." Phae gave Izzy a smile. "I'm glad I was here for you. That is the main reason your dad wanted me here. He was worried about you being alone the first time back."

Izzy gulped and sniffed. "I should have guessed. Dad was like that."

"Yes, he is a thoughtful person even though sometimes he makes mistakes. But don't we all."

Izzy watched Phae turn and move toward the door. She saw her wince and limp as she took her first steps.

"Phae, you're limping. Sit down. Is it broken?"

"I think it's just sprained. I'll be okay. How about I go fix us something to eat?"

"I'll help you downstairs, and we'll get some ice on your ankle. I'll make us something to eat." They made their way to the kitchen.

Phae was feeling uncomfortable having Izzy wait on her. She tapped the tabletop repeatedly and fidgeted, not knowing what to do with herself. She'd never had anyone wait on her. "You don't need to do this."

Izzy got a baggie, filled it with ice, wrapped it in a towel, and handed it to Phae. She then pulled out a step stool. "Here, rest your foot on this."

Phae smiled at Izzy as she thought about how much the young woman resembled her father. She had the same dark hair and blue-gray eyes and was a little bossy, like Finn. She watched as Izzy pulled ingredients out of the refrigerator preparing to make grilled cheese sandwiches.

Phae tried to imagine what Izzy thought about a stranger in her home. She cleared her throat. "Your father told me about your mother and how he sent you away."

She waited for Izzy to say something. Tension lingered in the air. "I'm not trying to pry into your life. I just wanted to let you know that I know."

Phae noticed that Izzy halted in her task and glanced up at the ceiling before she finished making the sandwiches. "What would you like to drink?" she asked after a moment's silence.

"Iced tea would be excellent."

Izzy set the plates and drinks down at the table and seated herself. She bit into her sandwich and let out a satisfied groan.

"Because he confessed, is that supposed to compel me to forgive him?"

Phae noted Izzy's sarcasm and looked directly into her eyes. "No. It's not forgiveness or absolution that he wants. He wants to make things right between the two of you."

Looking at her sandwich, Izzy said, "How long have you known my father?"

"Not long." Phae shrugged as she realized Izzy probably wouldn't want to listen to anyone defending her father. Besides, she wanted to get to know Izzy better. "A couple of days. We had an unusual introduction." Inwardly she smiled at the memory of falling into his arms. Adjusting her foot on the stool, she said, "We both lost spouses, which made it easy to talk each other."

Izzy hung her head. "I want to forgive him, but… how do I let go of the bitterness?"

Phae was surprised by the question, and she reached out and touched Izzy's hand. "The two of you will work it out. Give it time and be open. Try not to judge."

Izzy looked up and gave Phae a smile. "I like you, Phae Carson."

"I like you too, Izzy Callahan."

They talked about school and what to see in Mallorca. Phae's senses told her that Izzy was still fragile and nervous about the visit. She wanted to keep things light and pleasant.

Phae chided herself for being so clumsy. With her healthy leg over the other, she waved her foot back and forth like a horse swatting flies with its tail. As much as the foot throbbed, she would rather be doing anything than sitting and feeling like an invalid. Depending on others was not her strong suit.

Izzy helped her outside so they could enjoy the sunshine and view of the sea. "What are you studying at college?" Phae asked.

Izzy lowered her gaze to the ground, and her lips produced a frown. Phae sensed something amiss; perhaps her grades weren't what she'd hoped they would be.

Izzy's voice wavered and became sullen. "I studied business and finance." With a derisive tone and a half smile, she added, "I guess I have my dad's genes. I hope to be an international financier."

Mention of Izzy's father made Phae think of the man who made her heart skip like a stone across a lake. "Yes, sometimes our gene pool decides our gifts and talents. I never had a chance to pursue my dream. I wanted to be an architect."

"Why didn't you?" Izzy asked.

Phae told Izzy how she'd married young and had children which had become her priority. Going to school had not been an option. She'd been a wife and mother first.

"I wish I had siblings." Izzy's cell phone rang. Pulling it out of her pocket, she looked at it and pursed her lips. She took a deep breath. "It's my dad."

"Aren't you going to answer it?" Phae paused. "The two of you need to talk sooner or later."

Izzy turned her back and with resignation in her tone said, "Hello, Dad."

Phae didn't want to eavesdrop on their conversation, so she focused on looking at the garden and the view. Every so often, she heard Izzy respond yes or no, and saw her shrug her shoulders. Phae prayed that this would be a beginning to reconciliation.

"Dad wants to talk to you." Izzy handed over the phone.

Phae gnawed at her thumbnail, hoping Izzy hadn't told him about her falling off the ladder.

"Hello… Mr. Callahan." It felt strange to go back to addressing him formally.

"Hi, Phae. How's everything?"

Butterflies formed in her stomach. She could hear the joy in his voice and assumed it was because he had spoken to Izzy directly. "Fine. What about you?" She could almost feel the static through the line, anticipating his response.

"It's a first step. We at least talked. I'll be there in a few days."

She detected a hint of sadness in his voice. Her heart raced at the thought of seeing him again, but slowed as the thought occurred to her that he might not want her to be there while he was visiting. "Would you like me to make arrangements at the hotel?"

Quiet drifted between them. "I'd feel better if you were there to act as a buffer if needed. Besides, I like your company." With amusement in his voice, he said "It'd be good to have someone who can cook."

With Izzy's eyes on her, she knew she had to watch what she said. "I would be happy to do that for you, Mr. Callahan."

"Thank you, Phae. I like it better when you call me Finn. I'll call you later to talk when there isn't an audience around you."

Her heart swelled with anticipation of a private call. Not wanting to reveal her excitement, she said, "That will be okay. Thank you, sir."

She flipped the phone closed and handed it back to Izzy. "Well, how did your conversation with your dad go?"

Izzy kicked the stones around in the dirt at her feet and shrugged again.

Phae wanted to hug her. Instead, she limped over and rubbed her shoulders. "The first step is always the hardest. Just take it one step at a time."

Phae didn't say anything else, but she couldn't quell the deep ache for Izzy's hurt. She decided to leave her alone to think. "I'm going inside to get some more ice and to get out of the sun for a while. Let me know what time you would like to eat."

As she walked away, her brain filled with thoughts of Finn and Izzy.

She shook her head and wondered how there had come to be so much misunderstanding and lack of communication. In a short time, she had come to think of Izzy as a second daughter. Finn made her want things that she had let go of a long time ago. He made her long to be sensual and, at the same time, afraid to lose her independence. She needed to protect herself. It would be way too easy to become emotionally invested in these two lost souls.

She entered the house and went to the kitchen. She peeled carrots and potatoes and seasoned a roast to go in the oven. She replaced the melting ice with fresh cubes and poured herself a glass of water. She took the glass into the great room, wanting to prop her foot up. She stared at the clear container of water. *If only relationships were as clear as water*, she mused.

Phae leaned her head back and closed her eyes. An image of Finn smiling filled her subconscious. He turned and put his arms out to Izzy, and they embraced. There were tears and half smiles. Phae approached them, and they welcomed her into their circle. Her heart raced. She was falling into a black hole. Losing herself. Losing her identity, her independence.

As if from a distance, she heard Izzy's distressed voice calling her. Phae opened her eyes slowly and saw Izzy standing in front of her.

"I'm sorry if I woke you. Seeing you so still frightened me."

"I guess I must have dozed off. You look unhappy, did something go wrong?"

Izzy twirled her hair as she paced back and forth. "Phae, I want to have a relationship with my father, but I just don't understand how he could've sent me away. I need to get a perspective on it."

Phae motioned for Izzy to sit down next to her. She picked up Izzy's hand and squeezed it. She let out a sigh. She didn't want to break any confidences, but, at the same time, she wanted Izzy to feel comfortable with her.

Weighing her words carefully, Phae said, "I don't know anything for certain, but based on some things your father told me, and my own experience, this is what I think. When your mom passed away, it walloped him. He was angry and depressed. He felt guilty because he'd traveled a great deal and had precious time that could have been spent with his family. I can relate to that feeling. It isn't just about losing a person; it's losing a life you were going to build together." Phae paused wondering how to phrase her thoughts. "He just wanted to escape the pain. He started drinking heavily to dull the hurt."

Izzy's head bowed, and she appeared to be studying the floor.

Phae touched Izzy's chin gently, lifting it so she could look her in the eyes. "He didn't want you to see him like that. His business started to experience some downturns, and that was when he realized he needed to sober up."

# Chapter Ten

*P*hae stopped talking and looked down at her and Izzy's entwined hands. She had hoped that Izzy would say something. But she hadn't. She glanced over and saw that Izzy's forehead was creased.

"My guess is that took place over four or five years. By then, you were becoming an adolescent." Phae smiled as she remembered her own daughter's teen years. "If you were anything like my daughter was at that age, you probably had the attitude that you didn't need to listen to or care about anybody. It was your life, and you'd live it without his help."

Phae heard a little snicker and saw the hint of a mischievous smile that signaled to her that she had accurately described Izzy's teenage years. "Fathers don't know how to handle teenage girls. My husband certainly didn't. I suspect your dad thought he had done you damage so he didn't blame you for hating him."

Sighing, Phae explained, "The distance between the two of you grew to the point you hardly talked or saw each other. You were busy with friends and school, and your dad didn't think he had a right to interfere."

Izzy crossed her arms over her chest. "I was furious with him," she sputtered. "I'd like to give him the benefit of the doubt, but it doesn't make sense, Phae."

Phae squeezed Izzy's hand. "I don't know why he did it. Maybe he wanted you to be around other girls your own age, and maybe he wanted there to be a woman who could give you advice as you grew up. Maybe he wanted you to be with your mother's family because he thought they'd keep her memory alive for you. Did your aunt and uncle have children?"

"Yes, there was Adam, who was sixteen, and Beth, who was twelve. They liked to tease me and pick on me. It was nice having an older girl to talk to, but when Beth turned thirteen it wasn't cool to have me around. Sometimes I would hear Aunt Marie and Uncle Connor whispering. I felt like they didn't want me there. Aunt Marie sometimes told me about how much she missed Mom and how things that I did reminded her of Mom."

Phae imagined a lonely, lost little girl feeling like she didn't belong anywhere. She sucked in her breath. "I made plenty of mistakes with my children. Parents do the best they can. There is no 'Parenting for Dummies' book, and it's even more challenging when you become a single parent."

Phae watched Izzy stick out her chin and wipe her fingertips across her cheeks. She realized she was trying to put on a brave front.

Phae recalled her own daughter's actions when her father had passed away. She had been "Daddy's little girl." Her father was gone, and she'd resented a mother who hadn't been able to fix it. Mark had always taken her side during disagreements. She remembered their first argument after he died. She could still feel the painful jab of Kera's words. *"I don't need to listen to you. You know I'm right. Dad always took my side."*

The words had hurt. She remembered how hard it had been to tamp down the urge to slap her daughter. Instead, she'd said, *"My husband, your father, is not here anymore. I am, and what I say goes, unless you persuade me otherwise. He took your side because he wanted to keep the peace. I am a single parent now. If you don't like my rules, then I suggest you find another home. I don't want you to go, but I will not be disrespected."* She shook her head to shake off the unpleasant memory.

Phae looked up at Izzy. "All relationships are hard. They're like plants; they need to be nurtured, fed and sometimes pruned to be healthy. Parents raise their children to let them go and hope they become stable, productive adults."

Izzy shrugged, and her lips turned down. "You're probably right. I'm being silly."

A shaft of uneasiness shot through Phae. Izzy was holding something back, but damned if she knew what. She didn't want to press, for fear the girl would shut down and close her out.

She inhaled deeply and closed her eyes. As she exhaled, she cleared away any lingering emotions from her face and voice. "I want you to think about something. You know your father is not getting younger. Do you want to hold back having a relationship with him until it is too late? If you think you have unanswered questions now, you'll have even more later."

Izzy's eyes grew wide, her pallor white. Apparently, Phae had stunned her.

Izzy stood up and turned away.

Phae sensed Izzy needed time to process what she'd just heard. Her own heart felt heavy with emotion. She was trying to provide comfort to Izzy, and yet at the same time show her the responsibility she held in bringing their relationship together. She hoped that Izzy would digest the conversation and feel hopeful about repairing her relationship with her father, enough to meet him halfway.

After dinner, Phae and Izzy watched television and talked off and on about the programs they were watching.

"Phae, I want to thank you for talking to me today. You gave me a great deal to think about. You also helped me to see things differently."

Phae let out a relieved sigh. "I hope you weren't offended by anything I said."

Izzy was sitting on the floor, one leg crossed over the other. She shook her head. "No. You were being honest, and you are correct. If something happened to my father, I would never have my questions answered. So, I guess mending the fence is more for me than for him."

"I think it is for both of you."

Izzy stood up and looked at Phae. "I'm glad you are here." She smiled. "I feel comfortable talking to you." She crossed her arms and gave a shrug. "I'll be honest. I was afraid of coming here where my early life started with Mom, but I think if she were alive... she would talk to me like you did."

"What a sweet thing to say. Thank you, and I'm glad I'm here, too." Phae yawned. "Oh, look at the time. I think I'm going to head on up to bed. I'll see you in the morning." She rose from the sofa and walked over to Izzy and kissed her on the forehead. "Good night, Izzy."

Phae was just falling asleep when she heard her cell phone. Thinking it must be her daughter she picked it up. "Hello darling, how are you?"

There was silence for a few seconds. "I'm all right, dear. How are you?" Finn asked, a suppressed chuckle evident in his voice.

Phae knew she was past the menopause, but her neck, arms, and face were hot. "I'm so sorry. I thought it was my daughter."

"Are you disappointed?"

Phae could hear the hopefulness in his voice. She was still reeling from hearing him call her 'darling.' "No, not at all."

"How is Izzy?" he asked in a worried tone.

"She is doing fine. It's been a little hard with memories coming back to her." Phae lay back down on her pillow.

"Thanks for not letting on that we are friends."

Baffled, she thought, *Is that what we are... friends?* She felt a tinge of disappointment. But did she want more than friendship?

Clearing her head, she returned to their conversation. "I wasn't sure what you wanted me to do, so I just spoke as employee to employer," she said meekly.

"Yes, I got that." She could visualize a smile forming on his lips. "I like it better when you call me Finn."

He stopped talking for a moment. She got the feeling there was more he wanted to say.

"I miss talking to you. You help me see things more clearly, and I don't have a problem with Izzy knowing we're friends... If we are?"

"One can never have too many friends." She chuckled.

"Phae?"

Her mind conjured up a vision of a sullen-looking Finn. "What?"

"Did she say anything about me?" he asked hesitantly.

"Ahh. You want to know if we talked about you?"

"You read me so well." He chuckled. "Yes. But I don't want you to break any confidences."

"Oh, I won't." She fluffed her pillow and tucked it behind her back. "Your daughter is very confused and needs to understand why you left her."

Finn's voice was grave when he spoke. She imagined him running his hand along the back of his neck, the way he did whenever he was troubled. "Yes, I figured that she would want answers. I'm not sure if I… have the answers she wants to hear." His voice sounded strained.

"Finn, just be honest. Speak from your heart and let her know you love her."

She could hear Finn breathing. She wondered if she'd said something to upset or offend him. Her voice was trembling when she asked, "Finn, are you there?"

"Yes, I'm here. Since you brought up being honest, I… need to ask you something." His voice was low and raspy.

Her heart thudded as she wondered what it could be.

"What is this between you and me?"

"What do you mean?" she asked, stalling to gather her wits.

"You know as well as I do." He softened his voice. "I enjoy your company, and I've told you I like spending time with you. Maybe I imagined it, but I need to know if you share the feeling."

Phae bit her lip, considering her words carefully. "Finn, I told you. I don't want any involvement. I want this job." She sighed, knowing that wasn't entirely correct. The truth was, she didn't know what she wanted. She was attracted to Finn. But did she want to give up her freedom to have a relationship with him? She didn't think so.

"Is that all I am to you… a job?" There was an edge of hurt in his voice.

She squeezed her eyes shut, feeling guilty for hurting him, especially when she hadn't been entirely truthful.

Her mind raced. "No. You're not just a job." Her voice cracked. It's just—"

"I don't want to put you on the spot."

She cleared her throat. She wanted him to understand why she was afraid to start a relationship. "I married young, at the age of nineteen. I knew very little about life, love, and marriage, but I soon learned it isn't easy. There should be give and take. I seemed to be the giver, and my husband was the taker." She paused to shake off a whisper of unease.

"He demanded I gave all my attention to his needs. We didn't have anything in common, except maybe a strong work ethic. Work was his focus and priority. The kids and I were to show the world that he had it all. He didn't enjoy spending time with us. I take that back. He liked to spend time with Kera, my daughter."

Finn's voice was gentle. "I'm sorry. I'm not taking his side, but men identify themselves by their jobs."

She shook her head as she continued with her explanation, each word bringing back painful reminders. "It wasn't the work or the job. He made a good living. We weren't rich, but we weren't poor either. it's that he was an angry person. Nothing made him happy. I would wash and scrub, and he'd tell me, *'If that's clean, then I'd rather eat shit.'* The kids couldn't leave a single toy out, or he'd be screaming at them. I quit talking to him about our future or dreams because he squashed them."

"Why didn't you leave him?"

She inhaled a deep, resigned breath. "Because," she gulped down the truth. "I had no money, nowhere to go, no job skills other than being a mom. I had already sacrificed enough of myself and I wasn't going to leave the comfort of my home. In my mind, I knew what I had to deal with, and could handle it."

"Oh, Phae." His voice was thick and guttural.

"I felt guilty when he got sick. I thought it was my fault he was angry. I wasn't good enough for him. When he died, I was so scared, and more lonely than I ever thought imaginable. I had to focus on getting a job. As time went on, I became more confident. I talked with a grief counselor who then referred me to a family counselor. I don't want to be caged like that again. I like you, Finn. I enjoy spending time with you, but I don't want to be in a relationship where I have to give up my freedom."

A silence gave Phae a chance to anticipate what he might say. She would understand if he changed his mind about wanting to see her. "Thank you for sharing that with me," he said finally. "I think I understand, but one bad experience doesn't mean all of them will be bad."

Silence vibrated all around her. Finn's words had a profound effect on her. A light-hearted feeling came over her, and she wondered if it was hope.

"Oh, and if you're wondering if you would have still had a job if you said 'yes', I would have respected that, too."

His tone had lightened. She felt herself relax a little but wondered where the conversation would go from here.

"I need to fix my relationship with Izzy. I know it's going to take a while. Perhaps we could find a little time to talk privately?"

Her pulse quickened. "Perhaps."

# Chapter Eleven

As tired as she was, sleep evaded her. When she finally drifted off, a dream kept her from restful slumber. She was running from Finn. They were laughing, and when he caught her, he rained kisses all over her. She felt the heat rising in her body, and she let go of her inhibitions, taking her clothing off in a seductive way. But each time she was at the point of letting him claim her, vines sprang up from the ground. Beautiful flowered vines would separate Finn from her. Her heart was racing as the vines entrapped her. Then she saw her husband standing near a thick wooden door. He looked at her and slammed the door. He turned and pitched the key into the woods. She cried out to him to let her go, to free her. Then she heard someone calling her. It was Finn—he held the key.

She sprang up in bed feeling sweaty. *Strange dream,* she thought, *but what did it mean?* Was Finn coming to release her, or had he merely taken over as her jailer?

It was 6:00 A.M. and she was wide-awake, lying in bed, her mind in turmoil. She thought she heard Izzy in the bathroom. She listened to a groan, and then heard Izzy being sick.

Rising, Phae pulled on her robe and opened her door. She didn't want to intrude, but Izzy might need help. She tapped on the bathroom door. "Izzy, are you alright? Do you need anything?"

Holding her ear to the door, she listened for an answer. "No, I don't need help. It's just something I ate that didn't agree with me."

"I'll make you some tea. Come down when you're ready. Okay?"

"Okay," Izzy said weakly.

Phae hobbled downstairs to the kitchen. She retraced the events of yesterday, wondering what it had been that had made Izzy sick. She couldn't remember anything that they both hadn't eaten. She sensed that Izzy was anxious about meeting her father. "It's probably a case of nerves," she mumbled to herself.

There had been a tone in Izzy's voice that caused Phae to feel uncomfortable. Some sixth sense telling her something wasn't right.

Phae's cell phone rang, and she glanced at it and saw it was her daughter. "Hello, darling, how are you?" As the words left her mouth, she mentally replayed Finn's response last night. The memory made her body feel warm.

She and Kera chit-chatted for a bit before Phae told her that Izzy had arrived at the villa and she wasn't alone any more. She could hear the relief in Kera's voice.

As they finished the call, Izzy entered the kitchen, looking sullen with trembling lips. Phae went over and sat down beside her. "Izzy, honey, what's wrong?"

"Sometimes I think about the things I will miss out on because I don't have a mom." She sobbed. "I won't have a mom to pick out a wedding dress with me."

Phae's heart skipped a few beats. "Are you getting married?" Phae asked excitedly.

Izzy raised her eyes and shook her head. "No."

Phae reached over and hugged her. "Oh, Izzy, who knows what the future holds for you. But I will tell you this. Your mom will be there in your heart, and she would be so proud of you now."

Izzy returned Phae's hug. "Your daughter is lucky to have you as a mom."

Trying to lighten the moment, Phae said, "There was a time she didn't think so."

Izzy pulled out of the embrace.

"What do you want to do today?" Phae asked.

Izzy perked up a little. "If you have a bathing suit, why don't we go down to the beach this afternoon?"

Phae grimaced. "I don't have one. Besides, I'd clear out the beach if anyone saw me in a bathing suit."

"Oh, come on. Let's go shopping this morning and we'll go to the beach this afternoon."

Phae was puzzled. "I thought you weren't feeling well?"

Izzy waved her hand, "I'm fine now. I'll grab something light to eat. I haven't shopped in ages. It will be fun."

Phae's hand trembled as she lifted the cup to her lips. She studied Izzy. While she appeared light-hearted, Izzy kept tucking her hair behind her left ear, a nervous habit Phae had learned meant something was troubling her.

Phae thought it odd that Izzy had gone from being sick in the stomach to wanting to eat. She knew Izzy was stressed about meeting her father, but she had mood swings too. While all of that could truly be the anticipation of events to come, Phae wondered if Izzy was pregnant.

Phae shut her eyes, imaging how alone the young woman must feel, especially if the only one she could turn to was a man who had distanced himself from her for years. But then, maybe Izzy was planning to marry the baby's father. Phae would have to wait until Izzy was ready to open up. But if her suspicions were correct, Finn was going to have one helluva roller coaster ride ahead.

Phae had mixed feelings. She was concerned that a baby would take away time that they need to rebuild their relationship, but a baby would be a joyous occasion and could lessen the awkwardness. She thought about when Kera had her first child and how she had leaned on Phae for guidance. She wondered who Izzy would lean on for advice and support. She wondered about the baby's father and how would Finn react when he came face to face with a young man who had taken his daughter's innocence. She rubbed her forearms. She wanted to see Finn and Izzy become a happy family.

On the other hand, if Izzy were pregnant it would show Phae how he reacted under emotional pressure. Would he get angry? Phae could imagine her husband's reaction. It would not have been pleasant for anyone.

Phae and Izzy went into town and shopped. Phae noticed that Izzy wasn't an extravagant shopper, and she chose wisely. Izzy didn't want to give Phae a fashion show when she tried things on, which helped to confirm Phae's suspicions.

They were walking through the women's section when Izzy stopped short. "This dress would look lovely on you." She put her finger on her cheek and slowly walked around Phae.

Phae stiffened. She felt like a small creature being considered for a meal. "What are you doing?" she asked nervously.

With an excited voice, Izzy said, "Phae, please let me give you a makeover."

"Why? What's wrong with me?" Phae felt her cheeks flush.

"Nothing is wrong with you. I… didn't mean to imply there was. I've done this for some of my friends. They tell me I'm pretty good at being able to highlight their positive features."

Phae looked sideways at Izzy. She saw her pleading eyes and thought about how lonely she must feel if she was facing a pregnancy alone. Phae tapped her lips, thinking it might be fun to have another woman's opinion. She and her daughter had opposite tastes. If her daughter had her way, Phae's apparel would be moo-moos and tent dresses. She didn't have any women friends that she felt comfortable shopping with. This time in Spain was, after all, about change and finding herself.

Skeptically, but with a hint of adventurous spirit, she said. "Okay, but I will make any final decisions. I don't want to buy a wardrobe that I'll hate."

Phae chuckled as Izzy clapped her hands. "First, we are not buying a wardrobe, just a few things." She twirled around and picked up the dress of inspiration. "Like this dress. With your auburn hair and fair skin, this emerald dress would bring out the green in your hazel eyes."

"Izzy, where am I going to wear an evening dress?" Phae squawked.

"You don't know. Maybe we will find you a date, and you'll go out to dinner." Izzy's voice held a scheming tone.

"I don't date," Phae said sternly.

She ended up purchasing the dress and a sundress and bathing suit. At Izzy's insistence, they went to a beauty shop. When Phae sat in the chair, Izzy pulled the band from Phae's ponytail and spoke in Spanish to the salon owner as they circled Phae. Phae fidgeted and felt as if butterflies were circling in her stomach. She watched in the mirror as they fingered her hair and moved her face from side to side. She hoped this was just a haircut and not the major surgery their glum faces seemed to imply.

The owner started giving commands to her staff in Spanish. Izzy grabbed a magazine and sat in the waiting area.

Phae didn't want to watch. She gulped as she felt and heard the clipping of scissors and felt the weight of her hair leave her shoulders. She couldn't see anything because they turned the chair away from the mirror.

After the initial shock of seeing her locks on the floor, she asked if they could turn her around to watch.

Granting her request, she watched with curiosity as they placed aluminum foil under strands of hair and applied coloring. She paid close attention to how they applied her makeup so she could do this herself if she liked it.

They whirled the chair away from the mirror again as they styled her hair. Anticipation was building in Phae's stomach. Finally, after several hours of being beautified, the owner motioned for Izzy.

Izzy gasped when she saw Phae.

"Oh my, what's wrong, let me see," Phae said.

Slowly they turned her around. As she looked in the mirror, she couldn't believe her eyes. Her auburn hair now held gold highlights. It was just below her chin with soft, delicate waves that emphasized her high cheekbones. Her eyes carried on the gold flecks and were bright with excitement. A rust-colored lipstick outlined her mouth. She looked at herself, and her mouth fell open. Is this what had been hidden? She felt feminine. Feeling attractive gave her a sense of self-confidence, and the confidence made her feel powerful.

Izzy was driving them home While Phae sat quietly, reminiscing over the beautiful day. She smiled as she thought of her new look. "Thank you again for the makeover. It was fun, and I love my new look."

"It was my pleasure," Izzy chirped.

She was still smiling, but her eyes held sadness. "Are you all right?" Phae asked.

Izzy's gaze held a nostalgic look, and her lip trembled. "It reminded me of the only shopping adventure I had with my mother. I was young, only seven; Mom wasn't feeling well, and she thought if we went shopping, she would look better, which would make her feel better. The transformation I saw in her that day left me in awe. My mother was stunning."

"I'm sorry."

"No need to be sorry." She smiled. "I'm glad we did this."

They pulled into the driveway, and Phae recognized Finn's car. *He must have decided to come back sooner*, she thought. Glancing over at Izzy, she saw her face go pale. She reached over and squeezed her arm. "Take a deep breath, Izzy. It will be okay."

Izzy looked over and put her hand over Phae's. "Thank you," she said meekly.

They exited the car and were leaning in to get their treasures when Phae heard the front door open. Her heart skipped a beat. She turned and saw Finn. "Hello, ladies," he greeted.

He glanced at Phae, his eyes traveling over her from head to toe. Her temperature gauge was out of control. The air conditioner in the car had made her cold. Finn's eyes washing over her made her feel hot. She sizzled when he stroked his chin as his eyes met hers with a sparkle of hunger and delight.

As she watched, the joy faded and was replaced with distress. She knew he was looking at her bandaged ankle. She recalled how he had cautioned her to be careful and stay off ladders. She lowered her gaze, feeling sad that she had caused him distress.

Phae breathed a sigh of relief when his eyes left hers and turned to Izzy. His expression of joy held sadness. He opened his arms. "You're not too old to run into my arms and let me twirl you around." His voice was rough with emotion.

Izzy hesitated for just a moment before she dropped her packages and ran to him. "Oh, Daddy!"

Phae watched as father and daughter embraced with cleansing waterworks. Her heart ached for both of them. Emotion rose in her chest, making it hard to breathe. A lump formed in her throat as she choked down a happy sob.

Several minutes passed before Finn put his daughter back on her feet. He held her away from him. "You're all grown up… a woman," he croaked. "I have so much I need to say to you, and we will talk. Right now… I want you to know I love you. I have always loved you." He kissed her forehead tenderly.

Phae turned and tried to hobble discreetly toward the house. "Here, let me help you with those." When Finn grabbed the bags from her hands, a current raced through her body, causing her to drop one of them.

Finn bent and picked it up. When he rose, she saw heat simmering in his eyes. After a moment, he turned, and she watched his tush as he walked up the steps and into the house.

Izzy offered her assistance to Phae, and Phae leaned on Izzy for support. "I feel a little relief now that we broke the ice."

"See. I told you everything would be okay." Phae tucked her arm around Izzy's waist and gave her a squeeze.

Izzy's voice was barely audible. "Thanks." They had entered the house, and Izzy said, "I'm thirsty from all that shopping. I'm getting something to drink. Do you want anything?"

"I'd love a cup of tea. I'll be back shortly. I want to freshen up." Phae noticed that Izzy looked very pale. "Are you sure you're okay, maybe you should see a doctor."

Izzy's face looked panicky. "No… no. I'm all right, it's just nerves."

Phae was left standing with her mouth open about to say something. Instead, she sighed and shook her head, hoping Izzy would open up to her soon.

She climbed the stairs and sought the comfort of her bedroom. Her foot was aching, and she needed to get it propped up. She gathered a couple of pillows and stacked them at the bottom of the bed, kicked off her shoes and plopped on the mattress. Placing her injured foot on the pillows, she laid her head back and dozed off.

When Phae didn't come down after thirty minutes, Finn became concerned.

He decided to make a fresh cup of tea and take it up to her. He was anxious to find out what had happened to her ankle.

# Chapter Twelve

Finn knocked on the door, but there was no answer. He knocked again, "Phae, may I come in?" At first, he thought she might be in the shower. He listened and didn't hear water running. Frowning, he wondered if she was alright.

He cracked the door open and peeked his head around. He saw the bathroom was empty. The glass door was ajar, and a breeze was coming into the room. His eyes scanned the area and he noted a few bags and her shoes on the floor. Like radar, his eyes stopped when he saw her lying on the bed with her foot elevated. He sucked in some air, squashing the urge to call out her name. He wanted a few moments to take in the sight of her.

Her auburn hair splayed out over the pillow, the recently added highlights bringing a glow to her face. With her hands crossed over her midriff, she was the picture of tranquility. Resting so peacefully, her ivory skin and plump lips reminded him of the fairy tale, Snow White. A part of him wanted to be like the prince and kiss her awake.

He remembered the taste of her lips. She'd tasted soft and sweet—a combination that had made him want to deepen the kiss. He knew from her reaction after their outing that she was not immune to his kisses. Strings tugged at his heart as he wondered what she would do if he kissed her out of her sleep?

Quietly, he approached the bed and set the cup of tea on the nightstand. He was anxious to hear what stunt she had been performing when she'd hurt herself.

After her near miss on the arbor, he feared for her safety. She needed someone to look after her, to protect her, and to make her happy. There was a part of him that wanted to be that person.

His hand moved forward as though it had a will of its own and his fingers gently caressed her cheek. She began to stir.

A gap in her shirt gave him a glimpse of the laced edge of a leopard print bra. He wondered if she had panties to match and whether her spirit of adventure carried over into the bedroom.

Her eyes fluttered open. He expected her to be alarmed when she saw him; instead, he was greeted with a slow, sensual smile. He didn't need any little blue pill to get him aroused.

Gathering his wits, he cleared his throat. "I knocked. When you didn't answer, I came in. I brought you your cup of tea." Finn felt like a schoolboy in front of the principal explaining his actions.

She glanced over at the nightstand. "Thank you!" she said in a voice deep from sleep.

Finn sat at the foot of the bed and picked up her bruised ankle. "Do you want to tell me what this is all about?"

He was fascinated by the way she lifted her hazel eyes to the ceiling and then lowered them to land on his face. With a wicked smile, she said, "No."

Finn massaged her foot and ankle. "I don't know what took my breath away more when I saw you. How utterly gorgeous you looked or the bruised ankle."

Phae couldn't breathe. His attention sent her pulse out of control. His gentle hands stroking her instep and the sensual glide of his fingers along the top of her foot made her want to cry out for him to satisfy her hunger. His hands gently rubbed from her calves to her ankle. When his hands traveled upward, she thought she was going to spontaneously combust. Her nipples had gone hard at the thought he would touch them. She could feel her femininity pulsing with desire.

"I hope the incident didn't involve a ladder?" he said menacingly.

When she looked at him, the blaze of fire in his eyes told her he knew what he was doing to her. If she didn't stop this, there would be no turning back.

Phae pulled her foot away and swung her legs around to get up from the bed. She saw the bulge in his slacks. The only thing she could think to do was run before she gave in to temptation.

She moved to take a step but pain shot through her ankle and she fell back on the bed. As she tumbled backwards, she knocked Finn off balance and he fell over, too. He quickly turned and held her wrist to the bed, pinning her down. She could feel his desire as he laid atop her; she saw it in his eyes. What shocked her… was how much she wanted him to take her. To slowly undress her and touch her all over.

She was breathing heavily, and licked her lips to moisten them. She could see his Adam's apple pulsing. His breathing had become labored. They were both in heat.

His voice was husky as he whispered, "Tell me what happened to hurt your foot."

***

Finn's heart rate kicked up a notch seeing her eyes filled with desire and need. He wanted to give her what she wanted. Then he remembered his promise to her. He couldn't break it and lose the trust she had in him.

"Never mind." He jumped up from the bed and made a beeline for the door. When he got there, he stopped. "I have to go or I won't be able to keep my promise."

Phae gave him a puzzled look. "What promise?"

"The one that I would not kiss you unless you asked."

"Ohhh. That promise." Her voice was soft and sultry and held a tone of surprise.

He started out the door.

"Finn," Phae called.

He stopped, not turning around.

"I'm not sure if I want you… to keep that promise."

***

Finn was sitting at the kitchen table twirling his glass of iced tea in his hand. He was afraid to enter any love relationship. He couldn't go through losing someone he loved again. And he sure as hell didn't want a one-night stand, not that Phae was that type of person.

"Dad! Dad!" Izzy said, snapping her fingers in front of his eyes.

He gave his daughter a smile. "I'm sorry, honey, I was thinking." He wondered what Izzy would think of his romantic notions.

"You look sad or troubled. Is something wrong?"

He wanted to be honest with her. "I'm a little of both. It was very hard for me to let go of your mother. We were so much in love, and I'm disturbed because I don't think of her so much anymore. Sometimes I can't remember the sound of her voice."

He picked up her hand. "I only have to look at you to remember what she looked like."

"Is that why you sent me away?" she asked, her head downcast.

Finn pulled himself up, "No, not because you looked like her. Because I didn't want you to see a weak man."

Izzy's eyes grew wide with surprise, then glanced down at their hands. "I would never think of you as weak." She struggled to get the words out. "When I was a little girl you were big and strong and at the same time gentle and kind. I saw it in the way you took care of Mom and me."

Finn watched as his daughter wrestled to keep her composure. She squeezed his hand tightly.

Izzy looked up, pinning him with her gaze. "You thought I didn't see when you carried mom up the stairs to bed. Or carried her outside so she could get sun and sea air."

Finn closed his eyes tightly as he tried to keep the pain from surfacing.

He felt the puddling of nostalgia in Izzy's voice soft and far away. "I remembered baking cookies with you." She giggled. "You were my bronco horse and I rode you around the first floor. You would pretend to get on your back legs like a horse and whinny. You told me to hold on tight and not let go of you."

She slowly rose and took a hesitant step so that she stood in front of him. "I tried to hold on to you, Daddy, but… you let me go. I don't know if I have what it takes to hold on now. I'm no longer a little girl."

As he kneaded her shoulders, he thought about all the events and things that he had missed. He'd missed holidays and birthdays, watching her become a teenager, a young woman, teaching her how to drive, he'd missed her first dates to proms and school dances.

How foolish he had been. He'd lost the opportunity to share memories they'd never get back.

He turned her around and lifted her chin so that he could look into her eyes.

His voice was choked when he finally spoke. "I can't take back the years and all the hurt I caused you, but I would like to try to create new and better times moving forward."

A breeze swept through the kitchen windows, as if it were clearing the air. She moved away from his grasp.

Izzy shook her head. "I don't know yet, Dad. I would like nothing better, but how do I know if at the next sign of illness, whether it is you or me, that you wouldn't pull away from me again?"

He stood there speechless, his shoulders slumped, his eyes dimmed. She had cut him to the core. The sickening feeling of freefall showed him just how badly he had hurt her.

She appeared to wilt; a deep sadness crept over her face. When she spoke, her voice was nothing more than a whisper. "I… didn't mean to be so cruel. I guess I still have lots of anger that needs to be resolved. I'm sorry."

He couldn't be angry with her. He deserved the cutting words. A deep sorrow filled every fiber of his body. She was right. How could she know that he wouldn't abandon her again at the first sign of trouble?

Finn cleared the lump in his throat. "You don't have anything to be sorry about. It's me that is sorry. I don't know what to do or where to go from here." He scanned her face, searching for some small sign of forgiveness. "Do you have any thoughts about how to mend our relationship?"

She gulped her water. Somehow, they had to put the past behind them.

"Maybe we just need to spend time together... find some common ground and work from there." Izzy walked back over to the table. "I don't remember the house being so dark inside. It feels old and lonely. I remembered it as full of energy and fun."

"The house is yours, Izzy. To do what you want with. If you want to live here, fine. On the other hand, perhaps you wish to sell it and use the money to buy a house in the States. Either way, I think we should consider some renovating. What do you say?"

Izzy looked at him sideways with her index finger on her cheek in the way that her mother had done when she'd had something on her mind. "Yes, it needs to be brought into the twenty-first century."

Finn smiled, and pride filled his heart. She might have her mother's looks, but she thought like him. "I thought the same thing. It needs to be modernized."

Izzy hesitated. "Dad, did you know that Phae wanted to be an architect?" Her voice held excitement.

"Yes, she told me. She also said that she had taken some courses, but never finished her degree. In fact..." He didn't get a chance to finish speaking.

"Dad, what do you think about asking Phae to help us with renovating the house? We could work on it together, and I like Phae. At least we'd have an opportunity to learn each other's likes and dislikes?" Her eyes held a hopeful look.

Air bottled up in his chest, and his heart skipped a beat. With a chuckle, he said, "I was about to show you some drawings Phae made. They were ideas she had for the house." He got up and walked over to the counter where papers and tablets were kept. Rooting around, he found what he was looking for. He picked up the sketchbook and laid it in front of Izzy. "Take a look at these drawings and tell me what you think."

Izzy turned the pages, mulling over each one, sometimes touching the pictures as if they were a precious piece of artwork. He'd had the same reaction to Phae's drawings. "These are excellent. She's captured the historical value of our home; it looks cozy and warm, but it has modern conveniences."

He nodded. Izzy had hit on something he'd sensed but not been able to verbalize. Phae had captured the essence of the house without sacrificing modern conveniences, like state-of-the-art appliances. "Yes, I agree on both counts. This is a project we could work on together."

At that moment, Phae walked into the kitchen. "I'm sorry, I didn't mean to interrupt." She turned around and started to leave.

"No, don't go. This involves you as well," Finn said. He rewound his mind to their brief intimate moment upstairs, and the heat of the sensual memory radiated in his groin.

He shifted his gaze to Izzy. "I've just finished showing Izzy your drawings. We are both in agreement the house needs renovating, and we'd both like your help with the project."

"Phae, your drawings are fabulous," Izzy exclaimed.

"This is your project, Ms. Architect. What is the next step?"

"Really, you want me to coordinate the renovations?" Her voice was full of disbelief as she looked at both of them.

***

Excitement was growing in the pit of Phae's stomach. She watched as both nodded their agreement. She knew Finn was making this possible. The knowledge made her want to run into his arms as Izzy had done earlier.

Instead, she said, "I think we should take a tour of the house with those drawings in hand. I'd also like to get a list of the things that are absolutely must haves and things that you definitely don't want."

She stretched out her hand to Izzy. "May I?" Taking her sketchbook, she looked at the drawing they had been discussing—the kitchen.

"Let's start here in this room." She paused and made a one-hundred-and-eighty-degree turn, tapping her pencil on the sketchbook as she looked around the kitchen. Her heart gave a tug as she thought about her home in the States. "The kitchen is the heart and pulse of activity." She smiled. "It's where families talk. My children did their homework at the table, and now my grandchildren color and use Play-Doh there." She gazed out of the window. "Holidays, we baked cookies together. As adults, we made a tradition of gathering once a month for a cook along night." She glanced up at Finn. "I like to spend time in the morning at the kitchen table praying and reading my Bible."

Finn smiled at her. "I agree, and I have noticed that here seems to be a place of retreat when I want to think."

Izzy looked to her dad and back at Phae. "Me too. I like talking to you here in the kitchen. It's just that it is so dark and old looking."

Phae cleared her throat and straightened her back, and with a big smile said, "We are about to change that."

Overwhelmed by the mixture of mounting excitement and fear, Phae felt a tingling in her chest. She remembered her husband telling her managing renovations wasn't a job for a woman and to get the nonsense out of her head.

"I see a modern farm kitchen with hewn wood cabinets and quartz countertops, the walls painted a latte color to remind you of where food comes from—the earth."

She looked up to gauge their reactions. "An overall neutral look with splashes of color for each season."

Phae flipped over a few pages in her sketchbook and drew three columns and labeled them "must haves," "no's" and "nice to have."

"Okay, who is going first? Finn? Izzy?"

Izzy and Finn looked at each other. "A new stove with a convection oven," Finn said. He and Izzy gave each other the high five.

Phae shook her head and smiled. She loved their playfulness together. After an hour had passed, the sheet was filled with ideas.

Phae put down her marker. "Phew, I'm exhausted, and we haven't even lifted a board." She stood up and stretched her neck, hands and arms.

"Me too," Izzy said. "I'm hot and would like to go down to the beach for a little while. Who wants to go with me?"

Phae had walked to the doorway. she could feel Izzy's eyes on her.

Then she heard Izzy's pleading voice, "Please, Phae, go with me. We did shop for a bathing suit for you." She glanced over at her dad as well.

"Don't look at me. I have work to do and calls to make." He refilled his glass of iced tea and kissed Izzy on the cheek. As he passed Phae, he stopped and whispered in her ear, "Do you want a kiss on the cheek, too?"

His breath on her skin sent shivers down her body. She could almost feel his lips on her cheek. She itched to give him a big hug for helping to make one of her dreams come true. Nevertheless, what would Izzy think if she saw her father share an affectionate moment with someone other than her mother?

Instead, she picked up a dishtowel lying on the counter and swatted him with it. "Don't tease."

The mirth in his eyes faded. "I wasn't teasing."

Phae noticed Izzy staring at her with a silly grin and felt warmth flooding into her face. Finally, Izzy said, "He likes you. He seems happier."

Phae shook her head. "He is pleased because you are here, and the two of you are building an adult relationship. He wants that more than anything."

Izzy shrugged. "Could be, but I think it's more about you. You're kind and easy to talk to. I know I enjoy your company." Izzy raised her eyebrows and gave Phae a smile. "I'm pretty sure my dad does too."

Phae felt weak at the knees, and a little bit dizzy… like all the pieces of her life that she'd carefully reconstructed after George's death were threatening to fly apart. She didn't want to make any more mistakes, and falling for Finn, no matter how much Izzy would like that to happen, would be a mistake. How did you tell someone you are too damaged from the past to move into another relationship?

Phae's mind was in turmoil, and her heart was in an uproar. It wasn't just that her husband had been controlling; he had let her know she was "a piece of work." How many times had he told her, *"Nobody else would want you? You're lucky I married you"*? The words still had the power to diminish her. She had learned to keep her thoughts and opinions to herself and to keep him and everyone else, including her children, at arm's length. It'd been safer for them.

Even her children had grown distant from her when they were young. She had encouraged it because, if George saw any attachment the kids had for her, he mistreated them as well. She hid her feelings and learned to get by without love. Over time, she'd come to accept that love was for other people, not her.

"Phae, are you all right?" She heard the concern in Izzy's voice.

"I'm all right. I thought we were going to the beach?" Phae said as she busied herself clearing away the glasses and the iced tea pitcher.

"Yep, I'll meet you here in ten minutes."

Once Phae was in her room, she breathed a sigh of relief, and her shoulders relaxed. Now that she knew Izzy would be okay with a relationship between her and Finn she had to be careful, so that neither Izzy nor Finn got hurt.

Phae removed her clothing and put on her new one-piece bathing suit. The v-neckline and back made her look slimmer. A green and gold floral sash crossed over the top of the suit and emphasized her ample bosom. She wasn't thin by any means and could stand to lose some weight, but at least her exercise routine of power walking and aquatic aerobics had toned her muscles.

She was thankful that Finn was not going to be at the beach with them. She hadn't been this scantily clad in front of a man since the last time she and her husband had sex. He had fallen asleep before he even rolled off her. It had left her feeling empty and unloved.

She knew she had to get out of this slump, to push these feelings down. It did no good to look back, but the hurt didn't go away. No matter what she told herself, she felt a yearning to love and be loved.

Being around Finn and Izzy, she felt included in their circle, not as if she was watching from the sidelines.

She picked up the picture of her children and grandchildren. She loved them dearly, but being away from them had made her see how broken she had become. It helped her to see all the mistakes she had made. Like Izzy and Finn, she had relationships to mend with her children. She recognized it, but she wondered if they did.

Phae closed her eyes and let herself imagine what life with Finn might be like. He wasn't afraid to show affection like George had been. Every time Finn touched her, she felt charged. George had rarely touched her and, when he did, it was more of a tap on the shoulder as if telling her "good job." In the bedroom, his touches were rough and hurried as though he was just going through the motions. Why couldn't she just let go and show Finn that she liked him too?

For now, they had the kitchen renovations that would force them to spend time together. She had at least four more months to get to know him and to be with him.

But eventually she would need to return to the States.

Phae was surprised that she wasn't as eager to go home as she'd thought she would be after being away from her family. Her mouth turned up a slight smile. She, Izzy and Finn had become a tight nucleus. She marveled at how quickly they had all bonded. Her life would be forever changed for having been a part of their family. She felt water welling in her eyes and a jab to her heart told her she would miss them.

She donned her cover-up and went downstairs to wait for Izzy.

# Chapter Thirteen

She was in the midst of gathering up her notes from the brainstorming session when Izzy bounded into the room.

"Ready?" Izzy asked.

It was the first time Phae had ever been to the beach. She liked the feel of the sand underneath her feet and the sun warming her skin.

Phae removed a beach blanket from her bag and spread it out. She inhaled the smell of the fresh sea air. She held her face up to the wind and let it sweep her hair. What an exhilarating experience.

Phae watched as Izzy lay on a floating device, drifting away. She felt serenity wash over her, and her heart swelled with gratefulness that she had the ability to see, hear and touch this beautiful place.

She pulled out her sketchbook and tried to sketch the kitchen using the suggestions they had made.

She couldn't focus. She stared out at the horizon, seeing the contrasting shades of blue where the sky and the water blended. She put away her sketching material and decided she would catch a nap instead. It was only in her dreams that she could let her yearning for love surface.

Deep down she hoped to satisfy her longing in Spain. She had been lying to herself about not wanting to be involved in a relationship. Yet further down, the fear immobilized her.

She lay back and closed her eyes. The hypnotic sound of the crashing of waves lulled her to sleep.

She could smell Finn's musky scent, his warm breath on her face, his lips urging her to respond. She let her tongue probe his... she wanted more, she could feel her body heating with desire and she moaned, not wanting to wake up out of this dream. Her body quivered with a growing need for more.

She reached up, drawing him closer, and his tongue went deeper into her mouth. She cried again, only this time his lips left hers, and she felt chilled. Slowly she let her eyes flutter open. Still in a haze of love, she opened her eyes to find Finn's smoldering gaze boring into her.

Phae was embarrassed and shocked to find that the emotionally charged kissed was real and not a dream. She cleared her throat to speak, but she couldn't form any words.

"Don't look at me that way." Finn's voice was husky. "Your eyes, your body, they tell me you want me. But your words say no. I get mixed signals from you." He sounded confused and frustrated. He sat at the edge of the blanket looking out to the sea, as if searching for an answer.

Phae sat up and followed his gaze. "Where's Izzy?"

"She went back to the house. Said she was tired."

"I should probably go back as well before I get burned." She gathered her belongings and stood to put her cover-up on.

Finn grabbed her hand. "Please stay. Explain to me what that kiss was about." Their eyes met and, in that brief moment, she saw the depth of his hurt. She got the sense that he wanted and needed to know what was going on.

She sat back down, biting her lip. She shook her head and breathed in the fresh air in an attempt to lift the fuzzy, drugged state of her brain.

"I must have dozed off. I thought I was... dreaming and I wanted to... explore the temptation."

It had been so long since a man had found her desirable, and it was as though her yearnings were no longer just symptoms of her overactive imagination. It was as if they were becoming real, and she wanted to feel them again. She was embarrassed by those feelings and his scrutiny of her. Her lungs couldn't seem to take in any air.

Phae raised her arm to shield her eyes from the sun. Now, she felt alarmed at the desire and intensity of his gaze, as if he was searching for an answer that she didn't have.

His expression held tenderness, but filled with desire as he let his eyes travel down her body. The grin held a dash of devilment, and she could almost read the wicked thoughts running through his head—or were they her naughty thoughts about how it would feel to have his hands touch and arouse her?

Phae wanted to get away, but there was no place to go except into the sea. "I'm… going to cool off in the water." She stood and walked to the shoreline knowing that his eyes were upon her, which made her body temperature rise.

"That sounds like a good idea. I'll join you." In a few long strides, he was beside her.

The current around her legs made her unsteady. Finn reached out and took her arm.

"I want to go out a little further and let the waves carry me," she said.

"Okay, but I'll hold on to you until you feel comfortable on your own." Walking hand in hand, they moved further out into the sea. She watched Finn jump up as the waves came in. The water was chest high, and carried him toward the shore.

She let go of his hand and jumped up as a wave came toward her. She felt exhilarated by the water and the rhythmic flow. A wave crashed into her, going over her, and the undertow pushed her forward until she slammed into Finn's hard body.

Her heart was pounding, and she couldn't catch her breath. Finn's strong arms lifted her up and held her tight against him. As she gazed into his eyes, she saw the scorching heat in them.

It surprised her that she was responsible for putting that look in his eyes. She felt powerful and in control and, at the same time, she recognized that Finn had given her that power and control by letting her decide when and how much they would touch and flirt, letting her decide the next steps and actions.

That kind of power and control was something she'd never had with George. George always kept her at a distance. He had made the decisions about when they had sex. *But making love?" Hardly*, she scoffed mentally. It was more like engaging in the sex act. With Finn, she could feel herself wanting to give him everything she had, but the fear of losing control to another person stopped her.

She sensed that he would welcome her caresses and let her initiate their lovemaking. But for how long would he be content to let her have the control?

He lifted her chin gently, as she parted her lips and swayed into him. He kissed her hesitantly, gently.  His gentleness made her want to let her tongue explore his mouth. She felt on the brink of surrender.

He broke the kiss. "Why do you do this to me, Phae?" He was breathing hard.

She saw something shimmering in his eyes. It was more than desire. It looked like… caring. It couldn't be love. She didn't know what love looked like, and she didn't want to think about what it would look like; didn't want to think about what would happen if he was beginning to fall in love with her.

Her hand came up and touched his face. Her breathing felt constricted as she looked into eyes that begged for her answer. Confused by what she saw and how to explain her feelings, she disentangled herself from his grip and began making her way to the blanket. "I'm not sure I know what you're asking."

He watched her unhurried movements as she dried her torso, lingering over her arms and gradually moving down to her smooth legs. She stepped into her beach cover-up, taking her time with the buttons. He was on the verge of moving her hands and clasping it for her the way he had buttoned Izzy's coat when she didn't want to go to school. His frustration was mounting, and he squeezed his eyes shut for a millisecond in an attempt to rein in his emotions.

"Quit stalling. I want an answer," he said. "You don't know what I'm talking about? I know I'm not the first man who has been attracted to you."

"No, you're not the first man. After all, I was married."

Her voice sounded wounded as if he had dredged up painful memories. He felt like someone had punched him, unable to breathe. The last thing he wanted to do was cause her pain.

"Truthfully, I've been thinking that, since I'm so far away from anyone who knows me, I might put a want ad in the paper." She turned her back on him, cleared her throat and said, "Something like 'Wanted, a night of passion and lust. No attachments.'"

Finn started laughing, but Phae didn't join in. She looked somber. He raked a hand through his hair. "You're kidding, right? You don't see the danger in doing something like that?"

Phae didn't say anything. She let go of his hand and walked away, leaving him standing there.

Finn broke into a jog to catch up to her, muttering to himself, "Advertise for a night of passion! Over my dead body, she will."

He reached for her hand and swung her around to face him but the words he'd been going to say scattered like seeds in the wind when he saw the mirth in her eyes and the hand over her mouth.

Indignation hovered in her voice. "That will teach you to laugh at me." She pulled her hand away. "I enjoyed watching you squirm."

"If you're serious about wanting a night of passion, I'll volunteer." He pulled her against him. "And I'll enjoy feeling you squirm."

Before she could say anything, he kissed her. His hands slid down her back, caressing, pulling her closer. Then they moved to her butt, and she squirmed deliciously against him.

Phae pulled her lips away. "I said I was thinking about it. I'm not ready yet." With a sly smile, she added, "I'll put your name at the top of the list for consideration."

He nuzzled her cheek, sprinkling light kisses. "How will I know when you're ready?"

She bit her lip, pondering the alternatives. "I'll put your shoes under my bed."

Finn chuckled, thinking to himself that he liked this playful, flirtatious Phae.

"And in the meantime… what do I do?"

"Be yourself, be my friend. Do what is normal, but wait to be my lover."

They had arrived back where their blanket was spread out and picked up their belongings to walk back to the house. As they reached the grounds, Phae stopped and looked at Finn. "Can we go on being friends for now?"

Finn didn't respond immediately. "If friendship is what you want, yes, I'll be your friend. Does that make you happy? If, or when, we became lovers, I would still be your friend. I would respect your wishes."

Phae licked her dry lips. "I know I've asked a difficult thing of you and, trust me… it is confusing for me as well. I like you a great deal. We have a lot going on with the renovations, and you need to spend time getting to know your daughter again."

Finn remained silent as he watched her fidget with her belongings. When she began twirling her hair around her fingers, he knew she was nervous and working up the courage to tell him something.

"Losing my autonomy is only one of many things I am afraid of."

"I wouldn't expect you to give up anything you didn't want to give up," Finn said. "Your independent spirit is one of the things that attracts me."

"I gave so much to my husband and kids that I forgot who I was, and I don't want to repeat that mistake. There is so much I have not experienced in my life, and I'm afraid a relationship would take away that chance."

Their steps slowed to a turtle's pace. "I'll tell you something I want, if you promise not to laugh at me again."

Finn flinched at the reminder that he had laughed at her before, and said, "I promise, I won't laugh at you."

She reached out with her free hand and grabbed his forearm. Softly she whispered, "I want to experience falling in love, finding my soul mate, knowing I can share my fears, dreams, and longings. Does that sound silly?"

He kissed her lightly on the forehead. "No, it is not silly. Most people want the same thing. I had it for a short while once and lost it. I want it again."

They put their arms around each other's waists and continued to walk toward the house.

When they arrived, Izzy was sitting in the kitchen searching on the computer. Her cell phone rang. She took a glance at it and muted the ringer. Finn couldn't help notice how she tensed as she put her phone away.

"What are you searching for?" he asked.

Izzy looked up. "Appliances, flooring and what not, for the renovations."

Phae walked behind Izzy to see the computer, their heads side by side. He heard their 'oohs' and 'ahhs', pointing at items and making comments to each other. His heart swelled with warmth and caring for the two of them. They were a talented force together.

"Dad, you should see these appliances, some we didn't even think about."

"That sounds intriguing. Refrigerator, stove, dishwasher and microwave, what could we have forgotten?" He walked over and gently lowered the lid on the laptop. "Let's discuss it over dinner. Can you be ready in forty-five minutes?"

Izzy and Phae exchanged glances. "Anything to get out of cooking dinner," they said in unison.

# Chapter Fourteen

Finn was waiting in the foyer as Izzy and Phae descended the stairs. When he saw the ladies, he straightened his posture. He felt such a sense of pride and need to protect these special women in his life that he wanted to roar like a lion.

Phae winked at Izzy. "I think he might beat his chest. What do you say?"

Finn thought about how full his life had become. He hadn't believed he could feel such love again. He was proud of the woman Izzy had become and of her forgiving nature.

He shook his head ever so slightly. Phae… her beauty, kindness and ability to hear his regrets over his treatment of Izzy. How she'd jolted him out of despair when she fell into his arms.

Izzy laughed. "Yep, he's going to start beating his chest any minute now."

"What are you so happy about?" Phae asked.

"I was thinking I'm the luckiest man to have two of the most beautiful women in the world to escort to dinner."

As they drove into town, Finn and Izzy told Phae stories about the little villages they drove through.

They arrived at the restaurant, where Finn had requested a table outside overlooking the Baltic Sea. While they waited for their drinks to arrive, Finn asked, "What did you find on the internet that intrigued you?"

"This beautiful Italian marble for the kitchen floor and some stainless steel appliances," Izzy replied.

Finn glanced over at Phae. "What do you think?"

"It is beautiful. I want to research it for durability. I'm concerned that it may feel cold though."

Finn twirled his glass of wine. "Maybe this will help. I need to go to Italy next week on business. Would you both like to accompany me? You could go shopping."

He watched as Phae's eyes opened wide. Her voice drenched in excitement, she said, "Oh my gosh, I would love it. Izzy, wouldn't that be exciting?"

Instead of responding as expected, Izzy lowered her gaze, making circles on the tablecloth from the condensation of her glass of water.

"Is something wrong?" Finn asked.

She shook her head. "Nothing's wrong."

Finn wondered if he had said something to trigger her mood swing from happy to sullen. "You don't seem very excited."

Izzy looked at her dad and then at Phae. "Why don't you two quit pretending you're not interested in each other?"

Phae who appeared stunned. "Izzy I don't want to come between you and your dad. You two have a lot of time to make up for."

"Phae," Izzy glanced at her. "Dad and I are working through everything. Believe it or not, I want him to be happy. He has been alone far too long… it's like we're a family, and I like it."

Izzy looked at Finn. "Dad, Mom would want you to get on with your life. She told me so."

Finn reached out to take Izzy's hand. "It's not your job to worry about me. It's my job to worry about you and your happiness. I thought going to Italy would help us get to know each other again."

"Dad, I do know you. You think I didn't keep up with what was going on with you through Aunt Marie and Uncle Connor?"

Izzy gave his hand a squeeze and smiled. "I don't need a trip to Italy for that. Honestly, Dad, I don't want to go. I could use some reflection time. I… have some things to work out on my own."

Finn glanced over to see Phae's reaction. Her hand rested under her chin, her brow wrinkled. He said, "You're still invited, Phae, if you want to go."

"If you're there on business, and I'm not familiar with the surroundings I would be a little intimidated on my own. I wouldn't know where to find a Home Depot."

Finn didn't dare laugh. He looked at Izzy and noted the twinkle of amusement in her blue eyes. Clearing his throat, he said, "Italy and Spain do not have Home Depot stores. There is Bicofer's, Castorama and Brico Centers. Those are do-it-yourself building and hardware centers."

A slow smile crept across Phae's lips. "How silly. I should have asked."

They all chuckled, and the tension evaporated. The waiter came to take their order.

"What part of Italy are you going to, Finn?" Phae asked curiously.

"Rome for three or four days, and a day in Civitavecchia. I think you would find it very nice. It's on top of a mountain and is a quaint small town."

She laughed. "How do you pronounce that again?"

Slowly he said, "Chih-veeta-vekia." Her eyes focused on his lips to decipher each syllable.

Their eyes locked as she tried to say the name of the city with him.

Izzy's voice pulled her out of her fog of attraction. "That is what I am talking about," she said. "I was ready to throw a blanket over the two of you to put out the fire."

Finn cleared his throat.

"Izzy, I like your father very much. I'm just not sure I am ready for a relationship."

***

It felt odd, not necessarily in a bad way, to be having this conversation with Izzy, especially in front of Finn. Phae was able to express her thoughts honestly, without fear of reprisal. She couldn't remember a time when she would have been able to have any type of personal conversation with George. His nose was always in the TV. He never heard or remembered anything she said.

Her son Jeffrey was like his father, in that he wouldn't pay attention either. She recalled a conversation from about a year after George's death when her car broke down. She could still hear Jeff's voice. *"I'm the man of the house now, Mom. I'll take care of everything."* He'd then proceeded to tell her what needed to be done so she could handle it. He hadn't been concerned with her well-being after all. Or at least not concerned enough to drive her around.

Kera would chide her for having foolish ideas at her age. She did have to admit that her daughter would eventually come around, once she was able to relate to having similar thoughts or feelings. Usually, their conversations were about what the children were doing and making a list of things she needed to do for them.

Phae mentally chastised herself. She was an adult; she didn't need her children's permission. What she wanted was their support, and for them to care about her happiness.

Phae could feel her heart pounding with excitement and trepidation at the thought of a trip to Italy. She sighed, her thoughts on her and Finn in romantic Italy all alone, perhaps sharing a bed. She felt on the edge of guilt—or was it shame—though she had no reason to feel ashamed.

# Chapter Fifteen

As they were talking, Izzy's phone rang. The young woman looked at it, bit her lip, then disconnected the call.

Phae wondered who it was that caused Izzy to get anxious every time they phoned. Maybe this was what Izzy had meant when she'd said she had things to sort out.

Izzy nudged Phae with her shoulder. "It would be an excellent opportunity for you to think about a relationship. Who knows, it may not be with my dad, but some hot Italian."

Phae knew Izzy was teasing her father more than her, but butterflies swarmed in her stomach. She was not sure whether Finn would see the humor.

She risked a quick glance in his direction. Finn's jaw had tightened, his brows knit together. She recognized the beginnings of a dark mood. God knew she'd seen enough of them with George. They'd begun innocuously enough, with someone saying something that he took as disrespectful. As long as they were in public, he wouldn't make a scene. Once they were home she would pay the price.

She didn't encourage Izzy's teasing, hoping it would blow over by the time they returned home. She thought she heard Finn suck in a deep breath of air, but she couldn't take her eyes off his bobbing Adam's apple.

After that, she avoided eye contact with him and fiddled with her napkin.

"Izzy, there is no commitment between Phae and me. It probably would be better if she got to know other men." He gave her a mischievous smile. "Then there will be nothing standing in our way. I don't want to hold Phae back from exploring anything."

Izzy's phone rang once more and she quickly stilled it.

Finn rubbed the back of his neck.

Phae's anxiety climbed, and the room suddenly felt suffocating.

The interruption permitted Phae to think through Finn's words. She realized she was being silly. She shouldn't let her memories of George ruin a budding relationship with Finn, or any man for that matter. She was not the naïve nineteen-year-old she'd been when she met George.

She chided herself. There was no reason for Finn to be upset, as they didn't have a committed relationship. Theirs was more of a tentative friendship with romantic overtones.

Nothing more was said. Phae and Izzy chatted about Italy—what not to wear while visiting, what places to see. Phae's tension dissipated.

The young woman's cell phone rang three more times in succession. Phae was aware that Finn had been watching them. He cleared his throat. He had undone the first two buttons on his shirt, and she noticed his neck veins protruding.

Phae tried to concentrate on Izzy's words. Nevertheless, the hair on her neck rose at the tension in Finn. She wondered what was agitating him… what he was thinking about. Something was definitely troubling him.

Perhaps he was weighing what course of action to take. His relationship with Izzy was still fragile. Would she resent him butting in? It wasn't the first time she had received similar calls in his presence.

At that precise moment, Izzy's cell phone rang for the fourth time in the past hour. She glanced at it, frowned then pushed the button to stop the ringing.

***

Tension climbed his spine and knotted at the base of his neck. It would be a mistake to ignore the calls and Izzy's reaction to them. Finn laid his fork down and stopped eating. "You seem to get quite a few calls that you don't want to answer. Is something wrong?"

"No, it's nothing. I don't want to talk to anyone." Her eyes squinted, and she gave him a *butt out* look.

"Would you like me to answer the next one and put a stop to these harassing phone calls?"

Izzy's eyes grew wide. "No. I don't need your help." Just then her phone rang again.

He stretched out his hand and gestured for her to give him the phone.

She shook her head emphatically. "No. I'll shut it off. He won't call anymore tonight."

"Who is he?" Finn asked. His chest was tightening at the thought that she might be in danger.

"Nobody. Don't worry about it," Izzy said and took a sip of her water.

Finn ground his teeth as he watched his daughter gnaw on her thumbnail. She seemed unaware that her swinging foot kicked him. She looked around the room like she were planning an escape. Silence danced in the air, and concern that someone was stalking her flooded his mind. He couldn't leave her home alone if there was some crazy guy harassing her.

His thoughts drifted to the many times he had left his dying wife home alone, and recalled how quickly her disease had progressed. Sometimes there was only a short window in which to make the right decisions, and failing to act swiftly could have had deadly consequences. "Izzy, I insist you come to Italy with us."

Izzy turned pale, and she wouldn't look at him.

He now understood the term *tough love*. Sometimes you had to be strong even if it meant risking making someone unhappy. He had missed being a father to Izzy when she was young. He'd not been there to clean up skinned knees or to protect her from boyfriends, but, damn it, he'd be here now.

He saw the beads of water pooling on Izzy's lashes. When she spoke, he heard the struggle to keep control and the anger rising in her voice. "I liked you better when you didn't care about me. At least, then I felt I had choices. Don't you think it's a little late to play father now?"

Finn felt the stab to his heart. He deserved her anger, but what was he supposed to do now? As a parent, he wasn't willing to ignore the fact she could be in danger just because she didn't want his help or didn't trust him to provide it.

He swiped a hand through his hair and glanced at Phae, wishing she would come to his aid. Instead, three trembling fingers covered her mouth, and fear shadowed her hazel eyes.

Izzy was glaring at him. He took a deep breath, wanting his daughter to understand. "I didn't mean for it to sound so domineering. I offered to put an end to the phone calls that are upsetting you. These calls have been coming in more and more frequently, and each time you become agitated. I'm still your father, damn it. If someone is harassing you, I need to know about it."

"I told you, no one is harassing me, Dad. Can we just drop it?"

Finn's neck muscles ached from tension. He needed to get away and gain some clarity before he made an even bigger mess of things. Frustrated, he rose and threw his napkin on the table. "Excuse me, ladies. I'm going to get a breath of fresh air."

When he turned to go, Izzy bowed her head, and a tear fell on her napkin. He tried desperately to check his anger, but the fear and disappointment were harder to disguise. He felt sick in the stomach with worry for Izzy's safety. He was angry that he had lost control and had been insensitive. Nothing would get resolved if raw emotions were showing.

Once outside, Finn took a deep breath. He realized he had come off heavy-handed. His daughter had admitted it was a man calling her. It was hard for him to think of his little girl having a boyfriend, let alone possibly an abusive boyfriend. All he wanted to do was protect her. He did not want to fight through her evasiveness to do it.

Finn didn't know which had hurt him more, Izzy's words or Phae's frightened face and trembling fingers.

He closed his eyes and rubbed his neck. He heard Phae's voice from behind him. "Our food has arrived. What do you want to do? Pack it up and take it home, or come in and try to recover what's left of the evening?"

He shook his head, unable to bring himself to turn around and look at her. "I don't know what came over me, Phae. I am very sorry." Letting out a whoosh of air he added, "I'm scared someone is trying to hurt Izzy. I know you've seen how much these calls upset her. What if this man is abusing her or threatening her in some way?"

He heard the click of her heels on the cobblestone pavement as she moved toward him. She put her hand on his arm. "I have to admit, I didn't recognize you. For a second, I thought George had been reincarnated."

"He was that bad, huh?"

"Actually, he was worse. He never would have recognized that he said or did anything offensive, and he *never* would have apologized."

When she finished, she turned her back on him. Finn wanted to see the reassurance in her eyes that she was no longer frightened of him and that she believed his apology.

"I am sorry. I didn't mean to scare you or Izzy. What should I do, Phae? I don't know how to be a father."

She turned and gave him a weak smile. "I've raised two children and sometimes I still don't know how to be a parent. The rules change as they grow and become adults. We all make mistakes. Don't be too hard on yourself."

Finn admired her strength and understanding. "Thank you."

"For what it's worth," she said, "you're correct. I have noticed those mysterious calls. It concerns me as well… though I have my suspicions."

Finn's heart thumped and a lump formed in his throat. "Is she in danger? What do you suspect?"

Phae lowered her gaze. "I don't believe she is in any danger. If it is what I think, you'll just have to be patient and wait for her to come to you." She took a deep breath. "Don't confront her. It could potentially hurt the relationship you have built so far."

Finn's mind was racing, but Phae's belief that Izzy was not in danger calmed him.

"We need to get back to her. She's sitting at the table alone." Phae turned to walk away.

Finn reached out and took hold of her hand. "What about you, Phae? What about our relationship?" He prayed silently that he had not destroyed their chances.

"I… I don't know what to say right now. I have a lot to think about." Sighing, she continued, "You need to come in and join Izzy and me."

She removed her hand from his, and he heard the click of her heels as she walked away. Gulping, he made his way back into the restaurant, feeling as though he was facing the gallows.

At the table, Finn noticed Phae talking earnestly to Izzy and brushing tendrils of hair from his daughter's face. His heart swelled at the tenderness.

Finn cleared his throat to alert Izzy that he was back. Unsure what to say or do, he sat down and looked at the plate in front of him. "This looks and smells fabulous," he said, trying to ease the tension that lingered.

Picking up his spoon, he started scooping chicken, peppers, and onions onto his tortillas. He folded the bottom up and then the left and right sides over. He raised the fajita to his mouth to take a bite. His eyes caught Izzy and Phae pushing their food around on their plates. He stopped and set the fajita down. "Izzy, I want you to trust me with whatever is bothering you."

Finn and Izzy locked eyes. "I do trust you, Dad. I just need to find the right time to talk about it, and I will when I'm ready."

Finn started to say something, but he felt Phae's hand on his forearm.

"Why don't we talk about something else?" she whispered. "You heard her. She will speak to you when she is ready. Let it go."

"You're right," he replied, realizing that trust worked both ways. He needed to trust Izzy when she said she was not in danger.

Finn lifted his hand from Phae's and reached for his daughter's. "I'm sorry I upset you. I want to protect you and reassure you that I'll be there for you no matter what."

Izzy gave his hand a squeeze. "I know that, Dad. I just need to get used to it. I'm not in danger."

They ate their meals amidst stilted conversation, trying to avoid the elephant in the room.

Izzy fell asleep on the way home, and Finn didn't try to engage Phae in further discussion. She seemed to be lost in her own thoughts. He didn't want to think about how badly the night could've gone if Phae hadn't been there. She had a way of grounding him.

Finn reached over, picked up Phae's hand, and gave it a squeeze. "Thank you for steering me away from making a complete jerk of myself."

"No problem. I'm the outsider. I have a different perspective." Phae paused as though she were reluctant to say anything more.

"I'm listening…"

She squeezed his hand before letting it go. "I see and hear how both of you are struggling with how to speak to each other, afraid to say something that will cause a setback."

Phae let out a big sigh. "I was thinking, if you two had been in each other's lives and there had been no rift, you still might have argued. Kids and parents fight because they feel comfortable with each other and not afraid the other will stop loving them. Strange, isn't it?"

She shrugged. "You and Izzy haven't really had a chance to deal with differing opinions. This is the first, probably, of many." Phae let out a little laugh.

Finn considered her words. "I guess. I never thought that a parent and child argued."

At that, Phae laughed.

They arrived home, and Finn called, "Izzy, we're home."

Phae heard Izzy's groggy acknowledgment. "I'm sorry I fell asleep, I'm tired."

They entered the house, and Izzy started up the stairs. She turned around and came back down kissed Finn on the cheek. "I love you, Dad. Don't worry."

Phae watched the father-daughter exchange.

"Good night, baby. I love you too."

"Thank you for dinner, Finn," Phae said. "I think I will retire as well."

"Thanks for being the referee."

She had the urge to hug him.

# Chapter Sixteen

As Phae reached her door, she paused. Maybe it was time to give Finn's daughter a nudge. She walked over and tapped lightly on Izzy's bedroom door. "Izzy, are you still awake?"

"Yes, come in. I guess I'm not as tired as I thought I was."

Izzy was in sweat pants and a big shirt.

Taking a deep breath, Phae said, "I wanted to offer you my ears, if you want to run anything by me before you share it with your dad."

Phae waited.

Izzy bowed her head and fiddled with her shirt.

"Sometimes having an unbiased person listen, and hearing your own words out loud, brings things into perspective so you can realize nothing is as bad as you are imagining it to be."

Izzy blinked several times to dislodge the moisture that had collected on her lashes. Her chin trembled. "I wish I had my mom now. I do need someone to talk to."

Phae sat down on Izzy's bed, patting the space next to her. Dejectedly, Izzy dropped down beside her.

Phae rubbed the younger woman's back, comforting her as she had comforted her own daughter through breakups, unsuccessful cheerleading tryouts, and an array of other minor and major disappointments. "Do you want to talk now?"

Izzy rested her head on Phae's shoulder. "I don't know where to begin."

Phae leaned back against the headboard to be more comfortable. Izzy scooted back, and Phae put one arm around her. She could only imagine the sadness Izzy must feel not having a mother to talk to about womanly things. After George died, she'd had the opportunity to have Kera to herself. They'd started having "girl talks" that strengthened their relationship. She sighed at the loneliness that jabbed her. "Just start at the beginning whenever you're ready. I'm in no hurry."

The first minute was deafening silence. "I have, or maybe I should say, *had* a boyfriend." Izzy heaved a sigh. "Luke and I met at boarding school. We were friends for six years." Her voice was soft as she reminisced. "We met again at college. Luke was a senior and I was just starting."

Her voice had a dreaminess to it. "You obviously like him very much," Phae murmured.

Izzy's voice wobbled. "I'm pretty sure I'm in love with him."

Phae remembered the moments when she had thought she loved her husband. It had been wonderful and scary at the same time. She'd never been in love before. He had seemed kind and caring and made her feel special. She recalled how queasy and uncertain she'd felt. When he'd told her he loved her, she had said it back, not knowing what else to reply.

Kera, on the other hand, had been confident there was no one else for her but David. They started out as friends and then one day it become love. Their relationship was based on mutual respect and trust. Kera once told her that she could tell David anything. Izzy's declaration sounded similar.

The hand that Phae was making circles with on Izzy's shoulder stopped. "Is he in love with you?"

Izzy sobbed. "I think so, but he has a great career opportunity, and I don't want to hold him back."

A lump lodged in Phae's throat. She remembered how lonely her life had been because George was career focused. He'd spent hours and hours away from home, and when he was with them, he grumbled about everything. She and the kids made too much noise, they spent too much on clothes and shoes and school supplies. He never wanted to go anywhere, saying he was away too much and just wanted to stay home. She had finally come to the conclusion that George didn't love her enough to cut back on his work hours. Work was his means of escaping from her and the kids.

"I'm pregnant." Izzy sobbed and turned her head into Phae's shoulder.

While Phae had suspected that was the case, it still brought butterflies to her stomach. She remembered how scared she had been in a similar situation at the age of nineteen. She had been married, but that hadn't taken the fear away.

"What makes you think you would hold him back? Did he tell you that?" A sense of déjà vu encircled Phae. George hadn't been thrilled with the idea of having children; he had wanted to wait until his career was established.

"No, he's never said that. If anything, he tells me I am the most important thing to him."

"I don't quite understand what the issue is then."

Drying her eyes, Izzy drew a deep breath. "Luke is all about honor and doing what is right. He had a job interview in Chicago. The job could jump-start his career. If I tell him I'm pregnant he'll want to get married and live near the university until I'm finished. He'd lose this opportunity." She stopped and sobbed. "I'm afraid he would end up resenting our baby and me."

Phae closed her eyes, gulping down the hurt that rose into her heart. George's words rang in her ears. *"I could have been a vice president or CEO if you had used birth control instead of getting pregnant."* Phae bit down on her lower lip. It was as if George was alive, in the room with her, taunting her. *"I have to work my ass off to support you and the kids while you sit at home doing who knows what. I don't have a life because of you."*

She could understand where Izzy was coming from. George had grown to resent her, and she had learned to tolerate his resentment and the abuse that stemmed from it. He had been right; she should have taken precautions, but she had been young and innocent. She had looked to him for guidance. Maybe if they had loved each other more, it would have been different. "Ifs" and "could haves" weren't going to help anyone. She needed to give Izzy sound advice based on Izzy's life, not her own, and yet she couldn't help but think of what she would do differently if she had the chance to do things over.

Phae's stomach churned. The thought of Izzy so heartbroken made her sick. "Have the two of you discussed marriage and a family?"

Phae and George had never talked about what they wanted their life to be like or how many children to have, or when they would start a family. Everything had been by the seat of their pants. In fact, they had never talked much about anything that mattered. George only wanted to talk about his job and the people he worked with, criticizing everything. If she tried to show him a different perspective, he got upset with her.

She remembered overhearing Kera and David talking and making plans. When Kera got pregnant shortly after they were married, David had told her it was a change in plans but no big deal. He'd promised they'd still find a way to make their dreams come true. If only George had been the kind of man who was able to go with the flow and put their marriage first instead of his career...

Kera had been lucky, and it appeared Izzy was as well, to find partners who were their friends as well as their lovers.

"Yes, we've discussed it, but he wanted to secure his career, and I wanted to finish school."

Wretchedness descended over Phae. She and Kera had both gotten pregnant shortly after they were married, but their lives and marriages had been entirely different. George was self-centered and controlling. David was kind, giving, and dependable. Phae found him easy to talk to and loved him like a son. If Luke was cut from the same cloth as David, Izzy had nothing to fear.

As far as she knew, David had never resented Kera. He doted on their children and never showed one ounce of resentment. Sure, they'd had financial problems in the beginning, but they had talked and shared ideas. They had worked together and rolled with the punches, coming out stronger because of it.

Phae hugged Izzy warmly. "Well, the best plans need tweaking to get them right. I'm one who believes things happen for a reason."

Izzy shook her head. "I couldn't face him with this news until I sorted it all out. I ran away. Maybe I'm being selfish, but I'm scared." Izzy turned into Phae's arms and began crying again.

Phae closed her eyes, struggling to find words of comfort. Now the pieces were fitting together. She understood why Izzy had arrived in Mallorca earlier than expected. All the phone calls she hadn't taken, and her sadness every time the phone rang, now made sense. She felt guilty for not having approached Izzy sooner, but their relationship had been new, and they had been strangers.

"First, you're not being selfish. It takes two to make a baby. But don't you think you're being disrespectful by not telling him? Put yourself in Luke's shoes—how would you feel? You can't make decisions for him."

"Even if I tell him, I still have to tell Dad. How is he going to take this?"

"Izzy, let's take a deep breath. Dry your eyes. I'm going to get us some iced tea and then we'll talk this out." Phae got up from the bed. "Go splash some cold water on your face. I'll be right back."

Phae descended the stairs quietly and went to the kitchen. She didn't know what she would do if she ran into Finn. She wasn't a good liar, and he would start asking questions. And she had a tendency to become distracted when he was around.

She didn't need to turn on any lights because the full moon illuminated the space. Through the sliding glass door, she saw Finn standing outside on the patio, looking up. She poured the iced teas quickly and scurried back upstairs, wondering how Finn might take this news.

Izzy was coming out of the bathroom when Phae returned. Her eyes were still red and puffy, but she looked more in control.

"Feeling better?" Phae asked.

Phae handed her the glass, and Izzy took a big gulp. "Yes, I do. It's like a weight has been lifted just sharing it with you. Thanks." Izzy gave Phae a big hug.

Phae led her over to the bed and took the chair next to the nightstand. "How far along are you?"

Staring into her glass, Izzy said, "Three months. Are you disappointed in me?"

Phae leaned forward and patted Izzy's leg. "Why would I be disappointed? Babies are a blessing from God in God's time."

Phae leaned back in her chair, thinking about how she would've reacted if Kera had gotten pregnant before she was married. She couldn't imagine herself being disappointed. "The stress of keeping this a secret is not safe for you or the baby. You need a plan—one for you, the baby and Luke."

Phae and Izzy both yawned.

"Maybe we should save this for the morning when we're both wide awake and refreshed," Phae suggested.

Phae smoothed the covers over Izzy and brushed a few hairs away from the young woman's face. "It will all work out, you'll see."

Phae bent and kissed Izzy on the forehead. Just before she could shut off the light, she heard a sleepy whisper. "I hope you are right."

Phae shut the door. Once in her room and under the covers, she looked up at the full moon. She couldn't help but smile. *Imagine… Finn a grandfather!*

# Chapter Seventeen

The next morning, Phae woke with a slight headache from not getting enough sleep. She hurried through a shower and dressed, needing coffee badly. When she walked into the kitchen, Finn was pouring himself a cup.

He handed her the mug he'd filled and poured another for himself. She carried the steaming cup outside to the veranda. The light scent of the lemon and olive groves greeted her. She closed her eyes, letting the smell permeate her sleep-deprived senses.

"You girls were up late last night."

Phae opened her eyes, searching Finn's face to gauge what he'd overheard.

He stared at her over the rim of the coffee cup. "I couldn't sleep, and I saw the light on. It was after midnight." He grinned. "I thought Izzy was tired."

Phae gulped, not sure how to respond. She really wasn't a good liar, and she didn't want to break Izzy's confidence. There was always the truth, the whole truth and nothing but the truth… Instead she decided to go with the truth, but not the whole truth.

"I knocked on her door when I went up to check on her. She said she wasn't as tired as she'd thought. I went in, and we started talking." She held her breath. She had shared the truth; she hoped he'd drop it.

He looked at her gloweringly. "Did she share anything about the phone calls?"

Phae stared at the hot, dark liquid in her cup. She thought back to earlier conversations when they'd first met. He hadn't pressed her for information then. She rubbed her fingers against her chin. She thought about the times she'd run interference for her own kids—the secrets she'd kept from George to avoid him going off the deep end with punishment.

Straightening her posture, Phae set her coffee on the table. "Finn, think about the position I'm in. I'm Izzy's confidante, your… your… hell, I don't know what I am of yours. *Employee*? What your daughter and I talk about is none of your business. I will not break her confidences, just as I would not break my confidences with you."

She was breathing heavily, yet proud of herself for standing up to him.

He rose from his chair. His eyes held mirth, but his face looked grim. "I was only asking." He tilted his head to one side and looked chagrined.

She gave him her best look of determination.

"I'm concerned, Phae. I'm sorry." He took a step closer.

She felt befuddled.

"You're right on all counts, and I am sorry." His eyes narrowed. "I don't understand her reaction to those phone calls. She's obviously hiding something." He rubbed the back of his neck. "This is all foreign to me, and I don't know what to say or do, or what to not say or do."

She felt at a disadvantage with him towering over her while she sat at the table. She stood and took a few steps away as a means of calming herself.

"You're out of your element," she suggested. "You still think of Izzy as a little girl that you can tell what to do. She has her own life and while she may be dependent on you financially, you can't control her or tell her what she can and can't do. You have to let go. Let her learn from her own mistakes and be there when she comes to you."

"That's easy for you to say. You had your children with you through their childhoods, into their adulthood."

"Yes, I did. Nevertheless, I never really had any reign over them. My husband took control of everything."

The sound of the doorbell pulled them out of the heavy moment.

Finn looked over his shoulder at her as he moved to go. "This isn't over."

She heard raised voices, Finn's and a male voice she didn't recognize, so she raced to the front door.

"You must be the man who is stalking my daughter."

Izzy ran down the stairs shrieking, "Daddy, stop it. I told you no one is stalking me."

The young man shouted, "Izzy, what is he talking about? Who's stalking you?"

Phae's heart went out to both Izzy and Finn, the situation reminding her of all the times she'd run interference between George and her children.

Phae put two fingers in her mouth and whistled, much as she had when Kera and Jeff were small and had battled loudly over everything.

All conversation came to a halt. She walked over to Finn, placing herself between him and the young man.

"Hi, my name is Phae. I'm a friend and caretaker to the Callahans. You must be Luke. Izzy's told me a lot about you."

Phae's insides were tumbling, but she knew she had to take charge of the situation before things turned ugly. "Izzy, why don't you run upstairs and get dressed? Your dad and I will keep Luke company."

Izzy sent her father a warning look before she turned to go. Finn scowled at Luke and then at Phae.

Phae motioned for Luke to follow as she made her way to the kitchen. She could feel Finn's eyes boring into her back. "Luke, why don't you go ahead out to the patio, while Finn and I gather cups and make some more coffee?"

Luke went into the backyard while Finn stayed in the kitchen.

He scowled at her. "How the hell do you know about Luke? And why didn't you say anything about him to me?"

"I just found out about him last night. When Izzy is ready, she will talk to you. Now, go out there and… be nice."

Finn's face had turned thunderous. A knot tightened in Phea's stomach as she contemplated how this new rock scattered the pile. It saddened her to think he was angry with her for refusing to break her confidence with Izzy. She didn't like the feeling of betraying him, but either way, she would betray someone.

He looked up, and their eyes met. Suddenly she realized the distress in his eyes was not meant for her, but was a reflection of the mental anguish a father has for a child who might be in harm's way.

She gave him a half-hearted smile as the thought struck her that she wasn't afraid to take a stance or disagree with Finn. He was receptive to her ideas and suggestions. She suddenly understood that when Finn grew quiet during a disagreement, it was because he was digesting their conversation, not because he was building up steam getting ready to blow. If he disagreed with her position, he would gently and carefully explain his reasoning, always being respectful.

George, on the other hand, took it as a personal affront, accusing her of never taking his side, disparaging her with hurtful words—words that cut her to the quick, and taught her to keep her thoughts to herself.

Phae gave herself a mental shake. She didn't want to remember those dark times. She reached up and kissed Finn on the cheek. "Now go."

"What am I going to say? I don't know anything about him," Finn growled.

"Ask him about his job, hobbies he may have, or sports. Guys talk about sports all the time." Phae shoved him aside so she could get to the cupboard. "Ask him about his trip." She pushed two cups and saucers into his hands. "Take these outside. I'll be right out."

He gave her a slight smile, and she felt him relax.

Phae carried out the coffee, poured a steaming beverage into a cup for Luke, and set the pot on the table before she took a seat next to Finn.

"It seems Phae knows a lot about you, and apparently you know about me, but I don't know anything about you," Finn said arching his brow. "How do you know my daughter?"

Phae cringed at the edge of vexation in Finn's voice, and she felt sorry for Luke.

"Well, sir, Izzy and I became friends at boarding school." His puppy dog eyes lit up when he said Izzy's name. His deep voice softened. "Both of my parents died in an airplane crash when I was twelve. My grandparents thought it would be best if I went to boarding school. They weren't in the best of health and didn't have the energy to raise a young boy."

"That had to be tough on you," Finn said.

Phae's heart warmed at the compassion in Finn's voice. "I'm sorry I had to send Izzy. I thought I was doing the right thing, though if I had it to do over, I wouldn't have."

Luke gave them a boyish smile. "I'm glad you did, or I wouldn't have met her."

Excitement danced on his square-shaped face. "We became friends during those years. But we lost touch after I graduated and went on to university. During my senior year, I was helping with freshmen orientation and saw Izzy. Our friendship seemed to pick up where we left off."

Phae and Finn exchanged glances.

"I thought we had become more than friends." Luke lowered his eyes, and his voice sounded sad. "We were talking about getting married and having kids and building a life together. Then I went on a job interview that could get my career started."

Luke fiddled with the cup and saucer in front of him. "When I came back, Izzy was gone. Her clothes were all packed up, and there was no note telling me why. I tried calling her, but she wouldn't answer."

Phae noticed his eyes had become like liquid pools of chocolate, and he was massaging the side of his face. "I love Izzy. I want to marry her someday. With your permission, of course, sir."

Phae saw Finn's jaw drop and his eyes roll upward. She felt his tension, but at the same time, he seemed empathetic. George would never have given this young man an opportunity to speak. He would've slammed the door in his face and probably called the police.

"I decided if she didn't love me anymore, then she was going to have to tell me to my face. That's what brought me here."

"I appreciate your directness. Now I understand why you were calling her so much." Finn let out a sigh. "I guess if I was in your shoes and my lady ran from me, I would feel the same way." He paused and looked directly at Phae. "I would want her to tell me to my face to stay away." He drew in a deep breath and studied his hands. "But I didn't take my daughter for a coward."

Phae knew those words were intended for her.

"I'm not a coward, and I didn't run away." Izzy made her entrance. "I needed time to myself to think." She took a seat next to Luke and poured herself some coffee.

Squeezing Luke's hand, she said, "I am sorry. I do need to talk to you." She glanced at Luke. "Privately. Why don't we take a drive?"

Finn was obviously struggling to swallow the lump in his throat.

Izzy rose and bent down to kiss him on the cheek. "Bye, Dad. Don't worry, I'm safe."

Finn reached up and patted her hand that was resting on his shoulder. "I'll see you two later?"

"Yes." Izzy took Luke's hand, and they walked to the front of the house.

***

Finn took a sip of his coffee. Heaviness had settled in his chest. He noticed Phae was frowning. Several minutes passed with neither of them speaking.

"You're rather quiet. I sense from the look on your face you're thinking of George?"

She let out a heavy sigh. "Yes, I was. George would never have listened. He would've blocked everything out and ranted on and on that it was my fault."

"I think I'm in too much shock to rant and rave. There isn't anyone to blame when two people fall in love." He reached over and took her hand, bringing it up to his lips. "Not all men are like George. He sounds like he was a troubled and pessimistic man."

"I think you're right. I don't believe I ever saw him happy or content with life. But enough about George." Her foot started swinging back and forth. It was a definite sign that she wasn't comfortable with the discussion. "Will you give Luke permission to marry Izzy?"

Sighing, Finn said, "All I can think about is that we're finally getting to know each other again, and I'm not ready."

# Chapter Eighteen

Finn had trouble concentrating on what was being said on the conference call.

He stared at the picture of Izzy and his wife Angela, the last one before she passed. He thought about his daughter and Luke, how young they were, how uncertain life could be and how tragedies could change everything in an instant. It saddened him to know that Angela wouldn't be there for their daughter's wedding. He shook his head. It wasn't as if they were getting married next week. Luke had said, *"Someday."*

"Finn, what do you think? Can you make the day after tomorrow?" his business partner asked.

"I'm sorry, I zoned out for a minute."

"I was asking if you could go to Italy the day after tomorrow."

Finn glanced at his calendar, hesitating since Luke was there. "I'll make it work." He and his partner talked for a few minutes, wrapping up details. When Finn hung up the phone, he opened the French doors that led out to the private veranda and leaned up against them.

The trip to Italy was sooner than he'd anticipated. He hoped Phae would still be interested.

His thoughts rested on Phae. He mulled over some of their conversations and her reactions to various things. She seemed skittish and afraid to be touched intimately, yet other times she gave him that, "I want you too" look.

He walked through the doors and sat down on a chair that gave him a panoramic view of the hills of Spain and the Balearic Sea. A gentle breeze and the sound of the water relaxed him. This verandah always had a calming effect on him. He remembered how Angela had teased him about it when they bought the house.

Enjoying the silence for a few seconds, his thoughts circled back to Phae. No two marriages were alike, and everyone had difficulties. But he was curious about Phae's marriage to George. From what she told him, it didn't seem a euphoric relationship. She gave the impression their sex life had been more of a duty than a sharing of love and passion.

The way she always stepped in to calm the waters had to be the result of those years she'd lived with George. The way she put all her efforts into meeting other people's needs, and became contrite if they were not pleased, hinted at mental and probably verbal abuse, but he couldn't help wondering if there had been physical violence as well. It was clear George had instilled serious fears in her.

The way she reacted to his questions by becoming defensive, suggested the actions of someone not used to sharing thoughts and opinions.

He rubbed his forehead with his thumb and forefinger. Had they ever been playful or kidded each other? What had they done for fun? He remembered Phae saying they had never traveled or gone on a vacation. How stifled this must have been for her, who dreamed of flying and had hoped to be an architect. He wanted to give her all the things she'd missed. He wanted this trip to Italy to bring her pleasure.

He envisioned them strolling the streets of Rome hand and hand. They would explore the magnificent courtyards with fountains for tossing coins and making wishes. She was giving and loving and would do anything for anyone. He wondered what she'd be willing to do to give herself a relationship… travel… the things she'd dreamed of.

The fact she'd stayed with George also demonstrated she was loyal to a fault.

Finn thought about how concerned he was about losing Izzy. But he wouldn't actually lose her—she was his daughter after all. Truth be told, he worried more about losing Phae.

It was possible her children would soon insist she come home. He gathered from what she'd said that her son Jeffrey was a great deal like George, although Kera seemed to have more of her mother's wisdom and kindness.

Even if she didn't prefer to do what they wanted, he worried her sense of loyalty would compel her; after all, they were family. He wondered if she'd even think about what they could have together if push came to shove and she was confronted with a decision. Would she choose what would make her happy, or what would please her children?

He could feel the despair building in him. At times, the walls she built were so strong he could see the relationship doomed before it even started. But when she let her guard down, like with the kiss she initiated in the kitchen, he wanted to take that chance.

He went in search of Phae to talk about accompanying him to Italy. He found her in the kitchen, drawing and searching on the computer. She was unaware that he was there, so he took the liberty of watching her for a few minutes. She was graceful, her hair swaying as she moved, and the tip of her tongue jutting out while she drew. He hardened at the thought of kissing her, his tongue touching the pink tip of hers that poked out when she was concentrating intensely.

Clearing his throat, he said, "Hey there."

She turned around. "Hey. How was your call?"

"Good. That's what I want to talk to you about. I need to go to Italy day after tomorrow." He halted to take in her reaction. "I was hoping you would still accompany me."

She sucked in her lower lip. "Do you think that's wise now that Luke is here? It seems rude to have a guest and take off."

Finn grimaced. He was expecting her to be excited, not practical. "I can see if they want to join us."

He felt uneasy, as if she was keeping something from him. The barriers were up again. One wall down, two back up, he couldn't seem to topple them for good.

"I think that is wise. Talk to them first and let me know." She didn't look up at him as she studied her drawing.

"Is something wrong? I thought you were looking forward to going to Italy."

"I was. I guess Luke showing up changed things." She put her head down and continued drawing.

He stood there and watched her, frustration bubbling up in him. "I don't understand. One minute you take the initiative and kiss me, and the next you push me away." He inhaled deeply. "Help me to understand."

She sighed and met his gaze. "I can't help you understand when I don't get it myself. All I can tell you is I'm scared." She looked down at her feet. "I don't want to disappoint you, and I don't want to be disappointed."

He had to strain to hear what she said because she said it so softly.

He lowered his tone. "What makes you think you could disappoint me? So far, everything about you makes my heart skip a beat. You are warm and kind, and I want to give back to you what you have given me."

"Hello! Anyone here?" Izzy called. "We're back."

Finn's shoulders slumped. *Note to self: Tell Izzy her timing is off.* Seeing the mix of distress and profound sadness in Phae's eyes, he wished they could have finished this conversation.

"Dad, Phae, ahhh… could Luke and I talk to you in the library?" Her face was flushed, and she was doing that little side-step dance from one foot to the other like she'd done when she was three and knew she was in trouble for something.

Luke was pulling at the neck of his tee shirt, beads of moisture forming on his forehead.

Anticipation of doom took up residence in Finn's chest. "Is something wrong?" He looked from Izzy to Luke. The two squeezed each other's hands.

His daughter turned toward the library. "Are you two following us?"

Finn wondered what incomprehensible whims of fate awaited. He had a buzzing in his ears, and his hands felt clammy. Time seemed to have stopped. "Yep."

# Chapter Nineteen

Phae took a deep breath, feeling jittery and unsettled as she sat on the sofa. She wondered how Finn was going to take the news about becoming a grandfather. Would he be angry? She bit her bottom lip, worrying how Izzy would fare if things didn't go well. She felt uncomfortable with Finn standing behind her, and wished she could see his face and his reaction.

Finn placed his hand on her shoulder. She tapped it and said, "Come around and sit on the sofa with me."

Finn moved, and half sat on the arm of the couch. "Is that better? I feel at a disadvantage getting news when I'm sitting down." He made an effort to smile at Luke and Izzy. "What's this all about?"

"Sir," Luke's voice was barely audible and trembled. He squeezed Izzy's hand and smiled tenderly at her. Clearing his throat, he said, "Mr. Callahan, I would be grateful if you would give me your daughter's hand in marriage."

Phae looked up at Finn's face. She wasn't sure what to expect. She was used to flare-ups with George, and it still surprised her how calmly Finn took things. He rubbed his lips with his fingers and said, "It looks like you have her hand now."

Phae elbowed him. She was not amused by this little joke.

Finn looked over at Izzy, who shifted her weight nervously from foot to foot again. "Do you want to marry Luke?"

Izzy looked at the young man. "Yes, Daddy. More than anything."

Finn studied the two young, anxious faces waiting for his answer. He didn't know much about Luke, but he remembered Phae telling him that Izzy said he was all about honor and doing the right thing. That made Finn feel a little better, and he was glad Izzy had chosen someone she could respect.

Marriage and relationships were difficult, especially if you picked incorrectly.

He thought of Phae and what her marriage to George had done to her.

He had good memories of his own married life, which brought him back to the child he and Angela had created. How beautiful, intelligent, and caring. Their brief time together had already shown him how much she had matured. She was wiser than he had been at her age.

But they were so young; he wondered if they could handle the many changes that occur—building a career, taking on debt for major purchases like a home, cars, furniture. He grinned a little thinking of when children would arrive. Finn inhaled. They weren't the first couple to marry young. Phae had been even younger.

There wasn't much he could do about it. Izzy would be twenty-one in a few months. She didn't need his permission. She wanted his blessing. He needed to trust her instincts.

Finn reflected on the rocky start he had his father-in-law. The man had thought he was a gigolo. Finn remembered his words, *"What kind of man are you that you have not settled down before this? Are you a ladies' man?"*

He recalled how her father's disapproval had weighed on him and Angela. He wanted to be supportive; he owed that to Izzy and Luke. Luke had been there for Izzy when he hadn't been.

He walked over to the pair of them, took Izzy in his arms and hugged her. Then he gave Luke a bear hug.

Finn saw Phae move toward the group.

"Congratulations!" Phae hugged them both.

Finn turned around and went to the liquor cabinet at the back of the room. "Shall we drink a toast?"

Everyone nodded and Finn went about pouring glasses of champagne. "Izzy and Luke, I wish you love and happiness all the days of your lives."

They all raised their glasses and took a sip, except Izzy who lifted her glass but then called, "Dad."

Finn saw Izzy reach for Phae's hand. He wondered what was next.

"How do you feel about being a grandfather?"

The question rang in his head. *A grandfather.* A warm, joyous feeling washed over him. He stepped backward and leaned against the cabinet. He was at a loss for words.

Then the thought that Izzy might be marrying Luke because she was pregnant slammed into him. His mind raced with questions. Could they afford to raise a baby? He had already been a millionaire before Izzy was born. His career and business were flourishing. Luke's career was just starting. How was Izzy going to finish school? Would she have to go to work and if so, who would watch the baby? He rubbed the back of his neck. The thought occurred to him that if she didn't get married—and instead let Finn care for her—it would make up for the lost years. "Izzy, you don't need to get married because you're pregnant. You're welcome to stay here, and I'll take care of you."

He thought he saw Phae's jaw drop. He focused on his daughter and saw glistening pools in her eyes. He knew he had wounded her. She loved Luke.

They were young and wanted to make a life together.

"Izzy, I'm sorry. You asked me a question, and I didn't give you an answer." He blinked and looked again at her. "I would be ecstatic. I can't believe I'm going to be a grandpa." As he now stared at Izzy, he pictured her holding a baby and smiling—the contented smile Angela had worn when she'd held Izzy.

His vision became blurred as he thought about the last years and how lonely he'd been and how things would now change. The house would be full and noisy. There would be the sounds of a baby crying and happy gurgling of baby giggles. He caught a glimpse of himself holding a grandchild, walking and cooing just like he had with Izzy. There'd be no more empty and sad holidays; they would be filled with laughter.

Izzy ran to him and put her arms around him. "Oh, Daddy, I was afraid you would send me away again."

That statement startled Finn. Taking Izzy by her shoulders, he pushed her back to look her straight in the eyes. "Izzy, I will never send you away again. I've learned it's wrong to push the people you love away when you're hurting. You only end up bringing them pain and hurting yourself more. It's better to talk about the issue and the pain than to hide and withdraw." He pulled her back to him and held her in his arms.

"Thank you, Daddy. I came home because I remembered what a great Dad you were before Mom passed away. I want my child to be around you and to know you as you were back then."

***

Phae's eyes were clouding up. Her heart swelled with awe at how both were handling the situation. They may have been estranged, but they had taken giant steps toward mending and growing their relationship.

Her heart tightened with joy as well as sadness—joy for them, and sadness and regret for the years she had stayed with George. The realization that she had failed her children by remaining with a man incapable of showing love and compassion made her throat clench.

If George had been half the man Finn was, she wouldn't be harboring such regret. She must have pushed her emotions so far down she had barely been able to feel them because she was afraid to be hurt or criticized.

She'd had her children and a husband, but always at a distance. The reminder of the years of loneliness and isolation rushed at her. She felt claustrophobic, as though she couldn't breathe. Needing space and distance, she turned and quietly left the room.

***

Finn noticed her departure and sensed something must have triggered an unpleasant memory. He stayed a few more minutes with Luke and Izzy.

"Let's go out to dinner and celebrate," he offered.

When they agreed, he said, "I'll go see where Phae has gotten to. Why don't we plan to meet in the foyer at five-thirty?"

He left his daughter and Luke to search for Phae. He found her sitting in the kitchen. "Are you okay?"

She straightened her posture. "I'm fine. Congratulations!" she said and looked up with a smile.

He approached and took the seat across from her. "It's a lot to digest. I have mixed emotions, but overriding all of them is happiness and love. I never imagined this. I was so focused on the past and the mistakes and losses." He sighed. "This is like starting a new life..." Excitement rose in him. "A baby is a new life... growing inside Izzy. And I'm sure you're happy for them. But I saw you retreating and knew this must have triggered a memory of some kind." He reached out and took her hand in his. "I'm here if you need to talk about it."

She removed her hand from his, a sign the walls were coming up again. He felt helpless. He didn't know how to reach her. It felt as if he had slammed into a door and it knocked him off his feet.

"There's nothing to talk about. I'm just missing my family and seeing you all together, made me realize it."

Phae made eye contact. He searched her face, looking to see if that was all she was feeling. She broke the connection first.

Finn rubbed his face. He could feel her hurt, and it wasn't just missing her family. "Phae, we've only known each other a short time, but I've come to know when something is troubling you." He stood and looked out the window of the kitchen, seeing a bright blue sky and the sun slowly descending.

He was caught up in Izzy's and Luke's love and happiness. He wanted to feel like that again. To feel hopeful about the future, to know there would be someone at his side.

Unspoken words hung in the uncomfortable silence. The chair scraped the floor as Phae rose. "Luke and Izzy have good heads on their shoulders. They seem to know what they want. They have a bright, happy journey to embark on."

She took a step closer to him and touched his arm.

"I'm sure you're overwhelmed with all the news, but you're doing a fantastic job being supportive."

He turned and smiled at her. He was glad she was there to share this moment, even if she didn't want a deeper relationship with him. "We've decided to celebrate all this good news and go out for dinner. I came to tell you we will be meeting in the foyer at five-thirty."

Phae looked at him with a tentative smile. "I wouldn't miss it for the world."

***

During dinner, they talked about the wedding, baby names and a menagerie of other things. Conversation flowed smoothly and happily. As they finished dessert, Finn cleared his throat. "I need to be in Italy tomorrow by one in the afternoon." He glanced over at Phae. "Phae's under the impression it would be rude to leave you two on your own, as Luke's a guest."

Phae gave Finn a sideways glance to let him know she was not pleased with him.

Izzy squealed, "Phae, you must go to Italy."

Luke's eyes were downcast. When he lifted his head, he wore a frown. "Please don't let my being here keep you from taking advantage of this opportunity. I need to leave tomorrow myself. I have to get back to work to give my notice and start looking for a place for us to live."

She was touched by how gracious and concerned for her happiness they both were. She thought about how much she really wanted to see Italy. "Okay. I'll go. What time do I need to be packed and ready?"

"It's an hour and a half flight. The latest we should leave is 10:00 A.M." He signed the credit card slip and handed the plate back to the waitress.

They left the restaurant. Everyone was too full and relaxed from the meal to talk. It was a relaxed, comfortable quiet. When they arrived home, Phae said her goodnights and headed up the stairs.

It never failed to amaze her how easy-going and kind Finn was. Such a contrast from George.

# Chapter Twenty

She pulled out her overnight bag and packed clothing for the trip to Italy. Glancing at her watch, she saw it was 9:00 P.M. in Palma, which meant it was 2:00 P.M. back in Wisconsin. She telephoned her daughter. They talked about the children and what was going on in Kera's and Jeff's lives. She listened as Kera shared funny anecdotes about the kids.

"I'm sorry, Mom. I've been going on and on. How are things there?"

Phae told her about Izzy's news. Phae took note of Kera's intake of breath, followed by silence. She realized her daughter was probably miffed because she was giving attention to a stranger and not her. "Kera, don't be upset. Izzy's a young girl with no mother to talk to. She needed a female to discuss her situation."

Kera sniffed. "You certainly are getting involved in their personal lives."

Kera's words made Phae realize that she had come to think of Finn and Izzy as part of her family. When she was sharing her stories, it had felt like she was bringing Kera up to date with the rest of the family. It had given her a warm, happy feeling.

But Kera's response zapped her happiness. Her heart sank to the pit of her stomach. Sadness tightened her throat. The thought that it didn't matter because she'd find comfort with Finn and Izzy buoyed her. Then guilt reared its ugly head. Guilt that she didn't expect support from her daughter. She quickly tamped the feeling down.

She had nothing to feel guilty about.

She didn't want Kera to know how much her comment hurt.

"Perhaps," Phae's voice cracked. "But they accept me for who I am and what insight I have to offer." *And they make me feel appreciated*, she thought.

She closed her eyes and took a deep breath, bracing herself for more of Kera's disapproval.

"One more thing. I may not be able to talk to you for the next couple of days. I'll be in Italy with Mr. Callahan, shopping for items for the redecorating."

The cold silence that followed made Kera's annoyance clear.

Sparks of anger began in Phae's stomach and spread to her chest. Phae gave her shoulders a shrug. So, what if she didn't measure up to her daughter's expectations? It reminded her of how many times her own expectations hadn't been met.

She shook her head; how had the parent and child roles gotten so messed up? Her heart rate was increasing as she waited for a response. "Kera, are you there?"

She didn't want to argue when there was so much distance between them. She pursed her lips and reminded herself that Kera was her daughter, not her mother. *I don't need her approval for my actions.*

"Yes, I'm here. Don't you think it's improper to be going to Italy with your employer?"

Phae's temperature rose, and she could feel her head pounding from the thoughts racing through her mind. She clenched her hands into fists. In a carefully controlled tone, she asked, "Is it any more improper than when you and David were living together before you got married?"

Phae held her building anger tight. "We are both adults, and we will have separate rooms. There is nothing improper."

She knew she sounded curt and defensive, but she couldn't help it. She was disappointed.

"I don't need your approval; I merely wanted to inform you of my whereabouts. I think it best if we end this call now before either of us says something that we will regret."

She paused to give herself time to calm down. "I'll call you when I can. Give my love to everyone." She waited a few seconds to see if Kera would say anything more.

"Good night, Mom."

She heard Kera sniff and could picture the tears on her cheeks, but she was not going to cave this time. "Take care, Kera."

Phae disconnected the call and sat on the edge of the bed, feeling contrite, thinking about her children and their behavior. No matter how much she gave and compromised, it never seemed to be enough. There had been no pleasing George, and Kera and Jeff weren't much better. She rested her right hand on her neck, feeling her pulse, wondering how things had got to the point where her kids thought it was okay to pass judgment on her decisions.

She shook her head in dismay. It was her fault they were the way they were.

She didn't like conflict and had always tried to please everyone to avoid it. She rubbed her temples. She shouldn't have coddled them so much. She should've nipped it in the bud the first time her children disapproved of her actions or decisions.

In a way, she supposed she'd needed to come this far away to see how she had allowed them to stifle her. She shut her eyes and thought of the time three years after George's death when she had wanted to sell the house and move on with her life.

They wailed and carried on until she had agreed not to sell.

She remembered how embarrassed she had been when they'd told her, in the presence of her friends, that she was disrespectful to their father's memory if she went on a trip with their group. She still remembered the look of pity on her friends' faces and the hurt when they quit calling her to join them for dinner.

Her children didn't have any right to tell her what she could or could not do… or, for that matter, express disappointment in her. That was the problem; she should have told them when their behaviors were crossing the line rather than keeping the peace by giving in to what they wanted. She thought of the line "One can't keep doing the same things and expect a different outcome."

She sat there for ten minutes pondering her life and how she'd always given into George and the kids' disappointment, giving up the things she wanted to avoid conflict. No wonder they treated her the way they did.

It needed to stop, and it had to start with her. She was no longer willing to take the blame when things went wrong, or to give up the things she wanted to do to keep the peace. She would no longer take the easy way, suppressing her wishes to avoid conflict.

She frowned as she thought about the way she had spoken to Kera. But she wasn't sorry. Letting her daughter know she was tired of being on the receiving end of disapproval was long overdue. It actually felt good to express her feelings.

Tonight had been a first step. She sighed as she slipped her pretty nightie over her head and crawled under the sheets.

She lay there looking at the moon before she closed her eyes. Once more, dreams prevented her from sleeping well. In those visions, she was suffocating, and George was chasing her. He wanted to lock her in a cage.

She woke up startled and breathing heavy, just as George was about to toss the key to the cage in the ocean.

# Chapter Twenty-one

Her hands were shaking, and her nightclothes were damp. She got up and changed, drank some water and crawled back into bed. She glanced at the bedside clock. It was only one-thirty. The thought crossed her mind that, twelve hours from now, she would be in Rome.

She closed her eyes and this time saw Finn's face smiling at her. She thought about how differently he treated her—with respect and appreciation.

Phae woke at first light and was surprised that she felt refreshed and energized after a rough night. She was as excited as a child going to an amusement park. She wanted to run, skip and jump. Her stomach felt like a cocoon of butterflies ready to burst.

She climbed out of bed, showered and dressed. She didn't want to wake the rest of the house so she sat outside on the balcony. She loved watching the sun come up over the mountains, waiting for the moment when its rays hit the water and the sea sparkled.

She thought about the dream she'd had the night before. She realized that it perfectly captured how she'd felt about her marriage. George had used intimidation to keep her locked in a gilded cage, and now she was allowing her children to intimidate her. It was as if he still controlled her from the grave, through their children. Last night's conversation had been the first of probably many to come. She still had to deal with Jeffrey, but she would do it when the time came. She was tired of being intimidated by those in her life.

"You're no longer here to disapprove of what I do or don't do," she whispered aloud. "It's over, George. I will no longer let you control me. And neither will my children. I'm going to Italy with Finn."

She went downstairs for coffee and found Finn standing at the sink, gazing out the kitchen window.

"Good morning!" she said brightly.

***

Finn liked the sound of her voice. Hearing it first thing in the morning sent a shiver through his heart. He turned and smiled. "Good morning."

He poured coffee into a cup and handed it to her. Their hands touched, and both looked up. He saw trust in her eyes and felt an immediate shaft of guilt. She had trusted him, and he had embarrassed and manipulated her into going to Italy with him.

Finn released his hand from hers. "Phae, are you okay with going on this trip today?"

She took a sip of her coffee. "I am. I woke up early and feel like an excited child."

He quietly released the breath he'd been holding. "That explains why you appear chipper this morning." He watched her sip her coffee. "The chopper will be here shortly."

He had to suppress a laugh as her eyes grew wide and she shuddered.

"Did… did you say chopper, as in helicopter?"

"Yep, it's the quickest way." He twitched his lips. "Are you scared?"

Her eyes were bright with enthusiasm. "I don't know. No."

"Good morning!" chimed Luke and Izzy as they entered the kitchen.

"I'm glad you're up before we left." Finn kissed his daughter on the cheek. "I was telling Phae the chopper will be here shortly. There's coffee on the counter, Luke."

Finn moved away from the group and leaned against the cabinets, watching the exchange between Izzy, Phae, and Luke.

"I'm so excited for you, Phae," Izzy said, and Luke nodded, telling her places to visit and cautioning her on various locations and shopping areas to avoid.

Finn heard the sound of the helicopter approaching. "We need to get going." He gave Izzy a hug and a kiss. He shook Luke's hand. "Have a safe trip back."

"Thank you, sir, I will."

Then he picked up their bags. "Phae, we need to go."

They all walked outdoors. Finn helped Phae into the chopper and jumped in next to her.

He couldn't take his eyes off Phae's face. She beamed. He liked the way she edged closer to him and leaned across him to see out his window.

They donned earphones so they could talk to each other, and he heard her whisper, "It's breathtaking," as they passed over the Apennine Mountains. The pilot explained that the mountain range stretched 830 miles and was the backbone of the country spanning the entire Italian peninsula and ending in Sicily.

Finn reached down and picked up Phae's hand. She looked up, and their eyes met.

She seemed different today... happier, more confident and relaxed. Her eyes danced with delight at this experience. He felt weak in the knees.

"Thank you," she said.

# Chapter Twenty-two

When they landed, a limousine was waiting for them. "We will be staying in the heart of Rome on Via del Corso, which is the main street," Finn explained.

Then he realized she wasn't paying attention to anything he said. She was too busy looking out the windows and turning every which way. Her enthusiasm and spontaneity were contagious. His mouth went dry, and he nudged her shoulder. His heart raced at seeing the pleasure he had given her. "Phae, are you listening to me?"

She turned toward him. "I'm sorry. There's a lot to see. I don't know which way to look first."

He grabbed her hand and held it. "We will be staying at the La Scelta Di Goethe. It is a luminous and peaceful place in the heart of Rome." He paused a moment. "It has a unique view, where you can almost hear a soundtrack of ancient history."

He continued, "There are two streets you'll be interested in—the Via della Croce, which in the early morning still seems like a village where all the artisans greet each other by name, and the Via Condotti which is more frivolous and fashionable, should you wish to purchase shoes or clothes."

Phae glanced out the window. "I may shop for some souvenirs for my family." It dawned on Finn that perhaps she had limited funds to use for herself.

"The hotel is within walking distance of some fantastic restaurants which we will visit during the next few evenings." Finn retrieved his wallet from his pocket and pulled out a credit card. "Here, treat yourself to something special to wear when we dine out."

She pushed his hand away, "I can't use your credit card."

He grabbed her purse and slid the card into the outer pocket. "I want you to feel like royalty while we are in Italy. Humor me. Please."

She took hold of his upper arm and snuggled closer to him. "You already make me feel special. Thank you."

A lump formed in his throat at the affectionate display.

Their limo pulled up to the curb of the hotel, and the driver opened the door for her. A uniformed man came the door and introduced himself as Marco, then went about gathering their bags. They followed him into a private elevator.

"Marco is going to take me to my meeting." Finn squeezed her hand. "The limousine will be at your disposal whenever you want to go shopping for the tiles and carpet."

Her eyes widened, and Finn smiled at her. "Those shops are on the outskirts of town. You would not be able to walk there."

Marco chimed in. "I am pleased to be a tour guide. I know where the best home shopping stores are located."

"Thank you, Marco," Phae said and turned to Finn. "You think of everything. You're too good to me."

He had to suppress a laugh watching Phae's jaw drop as they entered the luxurious suite. Her eyes were drawn quickly to the wood-beamed ceiling and fireplace in the living room. She dropped her purse and slowly turned around, taking in the elegantly furnished suite. "We're staying here?" she asked in surprise.

As he nodded, he heard her intake of air. He was used to living in luxury, and he took it for granted. To see it from Phae's eyes was humbling.

Marco showed them around their suite. "The master bedroom has a terrace surrounding your space. There is also a two-person hot tub with a full view of Trinita Dei Monti, Villa Borghese, and the Vatican City."

Finn couldn't stop looking at Phae; she was every bit as beautiful to him as the view was to her. She practically bounced when she walked.

"The second bedroom has an equally exquisite view," Marco said and then left them alone.

Finn turned Phae around to face him. "I hate leaving you to explore the city on your own."

"Don't worry about me. I'll be fine."

But he didn't want to let her go. He wanted to stay and see where this new Phae was headed. He took her face in his hands and kissed her lips.

"I'll miss you," he said, turning and leaving before he couldn't bear to leave.

# Chapter Twenty-three

After he'd gone, Phae stood there touching her lips and thinking, *I'll miss you too*. The realization that she would indeed miss Finn shook her. She hadn't been alone in weeks; either Izzy or Finn had been close at hand. She hadn't minded. They'd had fun together, and conversation was easy. There wasn't the sense of always skirting the edge of an argument or disapproval like when she was with her own children.

She straightened her posture and reminded herself that she'd promised not to think negative thoughts, but instead to enjoy her time in Italy.

Entering the second bedroom, she looked around and didn't see her suitcase. She walked back into the living room in search of Marco and found him in the kitchen. "Marco, where did you put my luggage?"

"In the master bedroom, miss."

Phae went to the larger bedroom with the intention of retrieving her bag. She looked around the room and thought about what a romantic place it was. She picked up her luggage and stopped, taking in the tasteful decoration, the hot tub, and panoramic view. Her daughter's words rang in her ears, *"It's rather improper."* Phae bit her lip. She always did what was proper. She acquiesced to everyone. She knew Finn wanted more from her. What she didn't know was whether she was tempted because it was her nature to want to make people happy, or whether she was tempted because she wanted to be touched, to feel desirable.

She closed her eyes and sighed. Or was it that she wanted to feel the sexual pleasure that she'd heard and read about but never experienced?

She looked around the room once more, gripped the bag tighter and trotted to the second bedroom. She unpacked and freshened up. She had enjoyed the quiet moments in her own company, dreaming and fantasizing about sharing this gorgeous suite with Finn. Now she felt restless and antsy. She needed to get out and walk to release her pent-up frustration.

Her thoughts disturbed her. Thoughts of passion and lovemaking that she had let go of years ago because of George's cruel words. He'd called her frigid and told her he could get more satisfaction from a whore.

Phae inhaled deeply, gulping back the tears. Should she risk that kind of humiliation again? The thought made her heart pound.

She stepped out into the main street and looked left and right. It appeared there was a good deal of activity if she went left. She strolled about, window-shopping. She noticed all the couples holding hands, walking and talking. Sometimes they stopped for a quick kiss or to whisper something in each other's ears. She longed for those affectionate gestures.

She peered through the window of an elegant dress shop and saw a man sitting in the chair facing the dressing room. A dark-haired woman came out, wearing a tight red dress that hugged her every curve. The man motioned for the woman to turn around; the dress was backless and cut all the way to her tailbone. The man rose and approached her, caressing her shoulder, then nibbling at her neck.

There was such a sexual energy to their exchange; it was like watching a couple in the midst of foreplay. She closed her eyes and thought of Finn kissing her neck and touching her. She wanted Finn's eyes to desire her. She wanted to feel the same sexual energy she had just witnessed.

Phae stepped into the shop. The temptation to play with fire by purchasing something to fan Finn's desire took root.

A petite Italian woman asked, "*Posso aiutarla?*"

Phae didn't speak much Italian. She guessed that the woman had asked to help her. "Oh, no...." She urgently scanned through her Italian translation book to see how to tell the clerk that she had stepped in to get out of the heat.

The couple handed the dress to the salesclerk. "*Uno momento.*"

Phae looked at the floor. She heard the man whisper, "I can't wait for the evening to end so I can have the pleasure of removing the dress from your delicious body."

Phae gulped. In her head, she imagined her and Finn in the same scene. She wondered what her answer should be if Finn made that comment. Then she stopped herself. She didn't like that she thought about what her answer *should* be. She wondered what her heart would say.

She closed eyes and saw Finn's face and heard him whisper the words. She heard herself murmur, "What's stopping you?" She didn't like that it wasn't her style. She envisioned that she didn't speak. She reached up and undid his tie, then slowly unbuttoned his shirt, looking up at him with large, pleading eyes that told him to go ahead.

The couple left. Phae looked around the shop and found an exquisite emerald dress. It was made of a silky fabric that looked like it would flow gracefully. She imagined herself in this dress walking toward an astonished Finn. The clerk motioned to her to "*venire,*" to try it on.

In the dressing room, she held the fabric up in front of her. She removed her street clothes then slipped the dress over her head. Phae couldn't help the sigh that escaped her as the silk slid down her body caressing her skin. The cap sleeves were worn off the shoulder, leaving her bare shoulder to shoulder. The hem fell about two inches below her knees, and the fabric floated around her legs when she walked.

Looking at her reflection, Phae didn't recognize herself. The dress felt as if it was made for her. She pushed her hair up. It had been a long time since she had thought of primping for a man. She imagined herself in the dress walking toward an astonished Finn, his arms opened wide to her. While the dress revealed no cleavage, the off the shoulder look made her feel provocative and mysterious.

She decided to purchase it, along with shoes and a small handbag. Then she opened her purse and hesitated. The proper thing would be for her to pay for the items. Then if Finn didn't like the dress, he wouldn't be upset with her for wasting his money.

She could hear Kera scolding her about letting a stranger buy her an evening dress.

She hemmed and hawed, fiddling with the two credit cards. This was the twenty-first century. They may have an undefined relationship, but they were attracted to one another. If she didn't use his card, he would be hurt. If she did use his card, Kera would be disappointed in her.

Phae closed her eyes, then opened them to see the sales clerk's impatient expression. She heard a familiar voice in her mind. *"I want you to feel like royalty."* She smiled to herself and thought, *Let the king pay*, as she handed his card to the woman.

The sales clerk came around the counter and handed her the package. Then oddly the woman hugged her and said, *"Vorrei ti amo."*

Phae hugged the woman back. She didn't know what she had said, but it sounded beautiful. *"Grazie."*

# Chapter Twenty-four

As she opened the door of the suite, her cell phone rang. It was Finn calling. "Hello," she said cheerfully, "are you done with your meeting?"

"No. That's what I'm calling about. I have a few more hours here."

Phae's heart sank. She truly missed him. "Oh."

"Did Marco take you to find tiles?"

"No, not yet."

"I'll make this up to you, I promise."

Silence lingered. She thought about how much she missed him.

"I made a reservation at the Aroma for tonight," he said. "I hope you treated yourself to something pretty."

She enjoyed their little flirtations. "Possibly. I guess you will need to wait and see."

"I should be back around 7:00. Our reservation is for 8:00. I'm looking forward to hearing what you did on your own."

Phae heard someone calling him in the background.

"I need to go, Phae. I can't wait to be with you. Think of me."

*I think of him too much as it is*, she thought, reminding herself that she was in Italy to shop for materials for the renovation.

She phoned for Marco, and he drove her to Sorrento. There were several hardware stores and home improvement stores there.

She found several items she liked, but she wasn't comfortable making expensive purchases without Finn seeing her choices. After all, it was his house. He would have to live in it after she was gone.

The thought jabbed at her heart. How would she be able to live without him when she was already missing him after five hours?

# Chapter Twenty-five

Finn arrived back earlier than he thought he would. He changed and waited on the living room balcony for Phae who had been in the shower. As he admired the view, he thought about how much he had missed her.

He heard the second bedroom door open, so he turned to smile at her as she stepped through.

Finn's mouth went dry, and he couldn't speak. He could only think how beautiful she looked. The emerald color brought out the green in her eyes and made him want to caress her creamy unblemished skin.

"Say something, Finn." She bit her bottom lip. "Is this okay to wear?"

"I can't put into words how absolutely gorgeous you are." He crossed the balcony and came to her "I'm afraid to touch you; you might be a figment of my imagination."

She smiled. "That wasn't what I was going for." Her eyes twinkled mischievously.

He was speechless, letting her words seep into his brain. He wondered if she'd had a few glasses of wine to dispel her usual inhibitions. Nonetheless, she'd given him an opening, and he wasn't one to ignore an opportunity.

"Don't fret. I intend to touch you, caress you and let everyone in Rome know that you are with me." He moved closer, caressed her shoulder and pulled her forward until their lips met.

He had only intended to give her a soft kiss of affection. But when she opened her mouth, her lips were soft and welcoming beneath his, and the kiss became more ardent. Her hands rested on his chest, but as he deepened the kiss, they slid up around his neck. He hardened, and his breathing quickened. He wanted to be inside her. He wanted them to explore every part of each other.

As much as desired her, he wanted to give her more than sex in beautiful surroundings. He wanted to wine, dine, and romance her. He wanted to show her the passionate, sexy woman she was. He thought how ironic it was that George had had this woman yet only wanted a caretaker, while Phae was in his own life as a caretaker but he wanted the woman within.

He felt her fingers play with his hair. His hands cupped her face and then trailed slowly to her upper arms. He let out a groan and drifted away from her. "While I would love to pursue this path, I promised you some fun."

She bowed her forehead against his chest, and he noted her heavy breathing.

"Do you have everything you need?

Her laughter tinkled. "Yes. Where is it we are going?"

He had planned a romantic evening. They were in Rome after all, the city of love. The hotel Palazzo Manfred's rooftop restaurant, Aroma, had the best view. He had reserved a front row table with an unobstructed view of the Coliseum. He knew she loved architecture. The Coliseum was considered one of the greatest works of architecture and engineering and it always amazed him that it had been built by men with no formal education. He hoped she would feel the same sense of awe and wonderment that he did at the building that was ancient and yet alive, still captivating.

He took her hand in his. "While you are the most beautiful thing in this city, I thought we would do a little sightseeing and watch the sunset."

"Really? One of my favorite things to do is watch the sunset." She bumped into him gently. "Thank you."

He liked that she was letting her guard down. If she only knew how dangerous these little displays of affection were to his libido, he wondered if she would continue them. He hoped so.

She took hold of his arm and clung to it as though it were a lifeline. She looked up at him, her eyes full of yearning. He wondered if those yearning eyes and her hold on his arm meant she wanted him as much as he wanted her. Hoping to convey that he thought she was desirable and that he wanted her to be his, he let go of her hand and put his arm around her waist. "I like to feel you close to me. Is this okay?"

Their eyes met. "It's perfect." She returned the gesture and put her arm around his waist.

The elevator took them to the ground floor, where they left the hotel. As they strolled along Via del Corso, Finn explained that Italians had turned their daily pre-dinner stroll into the premier social event of the day.

"You're kidding me," Phae said.

Finn looked at the shocked expression on her face. He bent down and whispered. "Watch the other couples and tell me what you see."

She gave him a look indicating she thought he was crazy, then she glanced around.

People were in small groups laughing and talking. Small tables scattered the sidewalks where people would stop and share a bottle of wine or other drinks.

"It's such a babble of lively conversation. Everyone seems to be window-shopping."

Finn was enthralled by the bowled over look on her face.

"But is it my imagination? I feel like people are checking me out?"

He shook his head. "No, my dear, it's not your imagination. That is part of the *passeggiata*. Checking everyone out and being checked out—hence the Fendi, Gucci, and Armani clothing." He paused. "Everything in Rome is an art form."

They stopped and peered in the shop where Phae had bought her dress. She told him how she had used her phrase book to inform the clerk that the dress jumped out at her by saying, "*La mucca saltato sopra la luna.*"

He struggled to keep from laughing. He didn't want to embarrass her. He cleared his throat. "What was the clerk's reaction?" He hesitated a moment. "What you said was 'the cow jumped over the moon'."

She covered her face with her hands and shook her head. "No. Please tell me I didn't say that." Her shoulders shook.

Finn wasn't sure at first whether she was laughing or crying. He reached up to pull her hands away from her face and saw that she was smiling. He felt relief that she saw the humor in her faux pas.

When their laughter subsided, she said, "The woman in the shop said something to me and hugged me at the end, but I don't know what it meant. Probably she told me to wait there while she called the men in white coats to come pick me up, after saying something like that."

He smiled. "Do you remember what words she used? Perhaps I can translate for you."

Phae shook her head.

Finn took her elbow as they turned to cross the street to the Piazza Navona.

She nestled closer to Finn, her head tilted so the sun turned her red hair to a copper tone. "I can't believe the number of Ferraris, Alfa Romeos, Maseratis and Lamborghinis here. What happened to Chevy?"

Finn laughed and kissed her temple. "I love your innocence."

They continued strolling arm in arm. Finn enjoyed being with Phae; he loved her light heartedness and unruffled manner. He thought of her as a good friend, but sensed it was deeper than friendship.

They stopped at a little bistro for a glass of wine and an appetizer.

Finn studied Phae as she drank and ate. They held hands and talked about the different sights they had seen. She invoked in him a sense of chivalry he had not had an opportunity to practice. He had forgotten how much he enjoyed being the protector of a woman who was delicate and feminine.

His gut told him that he wanted more from her than a temporary fling. He could continue to offer her employment. But that would only be a pretense. He wanted her as a man wants a woman, all of her. He wanted to share a home, a bed and a life messy and blissful.

She had an enthusiasm and sense of adventure, and he liked that. He always knew where he was with her. She told him when he was messing up and tried to help him fix things when he made a blunder. As he recognized he wanted Phae in his life, he wondered whether she liked him as much as he liked her. He wondered whether she had given any thought to where their relationship was headed. He worried she might go back to her family. It was a choice he didn't want to think about.

"Do you want to walk some more?" he asked.

She squeezed his hand. "Yes. Thank you."

They meandered along the streets and climbed a steep slope in the Piazza Trinita Dei Monti. They stopped for some air halfway up. Finn heard a catch in her breath. Her eyes had wandered to the top where the late Renaissance titular church with its Gothic arches spanned two blocks.

He enjoyed the look of surprise on her face. Tugging at her hand, they finished climbing the hundred and thirty-five steps. Inside, frescoes by Masolino and paintings of the Virgin Mary adorned the walls. She held his hand tightly as he led her through the church and down a narrow stairway to the basement. Below was a second-century insula, complete with a shrine to Mithras.

In the past, Finn had visited this place when his solitude craved darkness. The sound of the water running to the Tiber had blocked out the painful thoughts in his mind. It had been a cleansing ritual for him. Water moving symbolized life, not death. It felt like the cocoon of the womb. He wanted Phae to feel the comfort of it too and wondered if she did.

"What's that sound?" Her face showed wonder and awe, her voice a husky whisper.

The stairwell was narrow, both sides made of rough, stone blocks. Finn felt her shiver and snuggle deeper against his side. He pulled her even tighter. "There is an ancient sewer that passes close by before dumping its contents in the River Tiber."

Entering the small insula, he watched as she stopped to caress the walls and ornate doors, her face reflecting surprise and admiration. There was a flicker of sunlight seeping in through the narrow window now turning her hair a warm copper. He stroked that hair, and he felt an overwhelming desire to hold her tight to take up where they had left off in the hotel suite.

Reluctantly he released her hand and moseyed further into the dark. "I want to show you something."

Phae was at his side in a matter of seconds. "What did you find?"

He cupped her face in his hands and claimed her lips, pouring every ounce of emotion and desire he felt into the kiss.

She gave in immediately, opening her mouth and fueling his desire for more. Her body relaxed against him, and she hummed in pleasure. She brought her hands up to his face.

He broke the kiss to look at her. Her hair was windblown and ruffled, and her lips were red and now swollen. Her eyes shone with passion. Her hands moved to the back of his head, and she pulled him closer to him. "Don't stop," she murmured.

She let her head roll back, revealing a long slender neck with creamy ivory skin. Drawn to her smooth skin, he began kissing her neck behind her earlobes. Her arms came around his waist, and her hands busied themselves pulling his shirt free of his trousers. Desire to feel her flesh against his coursed through him. Her hands caressed his lower back

His nostrils filled with the sweet fragrance of her perfume that acted like a drug, pulling him under the influence of her scent, touch, and taste. He wanted to touch her all over, to trail kisses over her warm, soft body. He wanted to explore what she liked and wanted in a lover.

He felt her hands leave his back and slide up his chest. She unbuttoned his shirt, and her long fingers played with the hair on his chest. Her touch stoked the fires within him. He let his tongue tease the seam of her lips. She moaned, and he eased the assault on her mouth. She was precious to him. He wanted to caress her, slow and soft.

He planted little kisses on her cheeks and eyelids. She deserved romance, slow, and steady lovemaking. He placed a gentle kiss on her lips and then bowed his head and rested his forehead on hers.

"I found the most beautiful, sensual woman and I want her in my arms and in my bed."

He didn't give her a chance to speak as he kissed her again. He could feel her heart pounding against his chest. She clung to him. His hands on her neck drew her closer, and he couldn't seem to get enough of her. Their tongues entwined, and he could feel her nipples hard against his chest. His heart soared at the desire he had evoked in her.

When Finn heard Phae's stomach growl, they both laughed. He eased away from her mouth and looked at his watch. He grabbed her hand. "Come on, we have to hurry if we want to see the sunset."

# Chapter Twenty-six

They walked to the back of the church where it overlooked the sea. Finn stood behind Phae, his arms around her waist. The sky was multi-shades of pink, orange and blue. Nestled among Roman cypress trees were ancient ruins and domed churches.

The setting sun displayed an array of color on the town and sea. The view of the Eternal City in all its glory was humbling. She leaned against his chest, her arms overlapping his. Words could not describe the feeling of awe and the gratitude to have eyes that could see this beauty.

The sun lowered ever so slightly, and the pink faded. They rocked side to side, a peacefulness sweeping over them. The sun descended lower, leaving an orange glow. Strange how, at descent, the sun seemed to get brighter. Or was it just the sky getting darker that made it look that way?

Finn kissed her temple, and she squeezed his arms tighter around her. The sun was resting on the top of the water. Half of the orb was no longer visible.

A breeze brushed over their bodies, warm and soft. The sun sank deeper still until only a sliver peeked out above the water. In an instant, there was a bright, white flash and the sea consumed the remainder of the sun. The sky went dark.

Phae and Finn continued to stand there. Everything was quiet, and it felt as though the world stood still. Slowly stars began to twinkle.

Finn had always enjoyed watching the sunset here. Even in his darkest hours, it had usually lessened his pain. It was the most serene place he knew. The way Phae rubbed his arms, he sensed she felt the serenity.

His thoughts drifted to Izzy getting married soon and moving away. His life would take on a new chapter. He didn't want this new direction to be without Phae. He didn't want her to leave, but he wondered whether she would be interested in staying on, not as a caretaker but as his wife. He wanted to cherish her, to love her, to spend the rest of their days traveling and being together.

Finn stood holding Phae. He didn't want to move and break the moment. It was as if they were the only two people in the world.

She continued stroking his arms, and they swayed back and forth.

It was his stomach that growled this time.

"Honey, do you think we should go eat?"

He blinked and felt a jolt of pleasure at her words. "Do you know that is the first endearment you've used?" His voice was hoarse.

"I'm sorry."

"Don't apologize. I liked the way it sounded. I could get used it." He squeezed her, turned her around, and kissed her. "I hope you've worked up an appetite."

They walked arm in arm down the Spanish Steps, still scattered with couples and groups of people. They arrived at the hotel and took the elevator up to the rooftop. The door opened, and a *maître d'* greeted them and escorted them to a table close to a bank of windows that looked out over the city.

Finn anxiously awaited her reaction to the view of the Coliseum. He wanted to absorb her pleasure and awe. He scrutinized her every movement, watching as scanned the decor of the restaurant, her eyes lighting up at the thousands of twinkle lights that illuminated the space.

He heard her gasp of delight and saw the widening of her eyes as she finally gazed down at the sight below of the Coliseum lit up against the night sky.

He felt her hand on his, her voice soft and full of emotion. "Finn, this is gorgeous."

He squeezed her fingertips. Finn remembered the first time he had been here. He had imagined the gladiators parading into the Coliseum.

Finn heard her sniff and saw her dab at her eyes. He played gently with her fingertips now. He wondered what was wrong. "I thought this would make you happy."

"Oh, Finn, I am overwhelmed. No one has ever gone to this much trouble for me," she gulped. "I don't know what to say."

"Don't say anything. You deserve to be treated this way."

She raised her hand and cupped his cheek. "Thank you."

He covered her hand with his and turned his lips into her palm. "You're welcome."

They held hands across the table, candlelight making everything appear ethereal. Their locked eyes spoke of love and respect, but not a word was uttered. He heard the waiter clear his throat.

"Yes, I'd like to order a bottle of Lazio wine. We will order our dinner a little later."

When the waiter left, Phae said, "It's like we are in another world."

"Yes. Think about the number of men who fought in the Coliseum for the love of a woman."

"Thank goodness we have become more civilized than that. I wouldn't want to lose you."

Finn caressed her hand, still playing with her fingers. "I don't want to lose you, either. Phae, we need to talk."

Phae lifted her hand and put a finger over his lips. "Not tonight, please. I want to savor the most romantic night of my life. I don't want to interrupt it with serious talk."

He took hold of those fingers once more, and one by one put them in his mouth, letting his tongue caress them.

She giggled. "I can't think when you do that."

Finn looked directly at her and formed a wolfish smile. "I don't want you to think. I want you to feel. To respond to my touches, to let go and be the passionate woman I know you are."

She gazed into his eyes. "I'm all yours."

He wondered if she really meant it. He was tempted to ask but didn't want to risk spoiling the moment. Instead, he raised his eyebrows. His voice husky, he said, "Be careful what you say. If I make you mine, I'll never let you go."

The wine steward arrived and poured some for Finn to taste. Finn nodded his acceptance. When the man left, Finn proposed a toast. "*Vi auguro un sacco di felicita e di amor.*"

He saw the surprise and curiosity glowing in her eyes.

"The clerk in the shop said something similar to me. What does it mean?"

He lifted his glass. "I wish you lots of happiness and love." They clinked glasses and their eyes locked as they sipped their wine.

# Chapter Twenty-seven

Finn ordered fresh artichoke salads and a classic Roman pasta dish. He told her about the underground rooms at the Coliseum where the lions had been kept, as they sipped wine and gazed at each other. They made small talk, reminiscing about the sights they had visited and talking about the things Phae still wanted to see.

"That was the most delicious meal I have ever eaten." She dabbed her mouth with her napkin and then set it to the left of the plate.

"I hope you saved room for dessert."

"I couldn't eat another bite."

He felt deflated, but he wasn't discouraged. "You need to try the *torta caprese*. It is a chocolate cake made with ground almonds grown on the island of Capri, near Naples."

He watched as her eyes rolled to the heavens.

"I promise it is light. Not heavy, like chocolate brownies or apple pie. Trust me."

She smiled at him.

He ordered one slice, and they shared it, feeding each other. Every time she opened her mouth and licked her lips, he wanted to reach over and lick her lips for her.

"Do you want to walk back or take a cab?" he asked as he fed her the last bite.

"I prefer walking to get some of this food burned away."

"My thoughts exactly."

They took the elevator down to the street and walked several blocks hand in hand. Music was playing, and couples meandered arm in arm through the Piazza di Spagna.

They were drawn to a group of dancers performing an Italian folk dance called the Tarantella. The female dancers wore brightly colored skirts, each a different color. White aprons trimmed with brightly colored ribbon topped the skirts, and white blouses and black vests laced up with the same ribbon completed the costume. The men wore black pants and white shirts. Their only adornments were red sashes around their waists.

The dance was very lively, with quick steps. As they watched the dancers, Finn was mesmerized by the excitement in Phae's eyes and her head bobbing to the music.

He leaned over, his lips close to her ear. "One legend has the dance going back to the 1500s when it was believed that the only cure for someone who had been bitten by a tarantula spider was wild and frenzied dancing."

Her expression changed from curiosity to mischief. She used the sheer silk pashmina she had brought with her and draped it around his neck. Using the ends, she drew him closer, her eyes sparkling with tomfoolery, the way they had when they were in the insula.

The spell was broken by the crowd's applause.

Finn leaned down and whispered in Phae's ear, "Do you want to go dancing?"

She looked over at him and nodded, smiling from ear to ear.

"Do you know any Latin dances?" he asked.

The wash of terror on her face replaced her smile and left him feeling guilty. "Don't worry I know a place where we can learn," he soothed. "The El Tocororo is a restaurant, pizzeria, disco and Latin bar as well as a dance school."

She looked at him skeptically. "Really?"

He chuckled. "Yes, really." He took her hand in his. "Many years ago, I took lessons there. It has been a long time since I have danced though. I could use a refresher course. No worries." He shrugged. "We'll learn together."

As they entered the El Tocororo, Finn hoped his friend Tony was still the dance instructor. They made their way through the crowd, and he recognized Tony and Celeste even from a distance.

He tapped Phae on the shoulder and pointed across the room. Pulling her close to him so she could hear, he said, "Watch the couple on the stage. They taught me to dance many years ago."

Her eyes dancing with joy, Phae beamed at him. He took her hand and together they made their way closer to the stage. Tony and Celeste danced, their hips swaying in unison as they touched one another. They teased each other… alternately touching seductively, then moving away from each other as if they were telling a story of attraction, loss and reconnection. Eroticism sizzled between them.

It was the way Celeste touched Tony's chest with a slight hesitation. Then the way he captured her hand and brought her back to him as she spun to leave him. Finn was always fascinated watching the Rumba, not so much by the steps, but the language spoken through the movement of their bodies. It triggered emotions and a deep sense of intimacy. He wondered if he would be able to convey his feelings for Phae to her when they danced.

Tony looked over at Finn and winked as he spoke into the microphone to enquire who wanted to learn the Rumba. He and Phae, along with several other couples, raised their hands. When Tony and Celeste left the stage, they ushered the couples who had raised their hands to a room in the back.

Celeste lined everyone up and showed them how to do a box step—slow, quick-quick… slow, quick-quick, emphasizing the movement of the hips.

Celeste instructed them to practice moving toward and away from each other. "The rumba is a mating and conquering dance. When couples move together, it becomes a mind, body, and spiritual connection."

***

Phae went into Finn's arms and pulled him to her. She rubbed herself up against him. Her movements were stiff and felt overexaggerated. It had been a long time since she had wanted to be sensual for a man and she realized she was trying too hard. Her breathing grew rapid, and she forced a deep breath.

Celeste came over, grabbed Phae by the hand, and stepped her away from Finn.

"You must let the man lead," she explained. "Look into his eyes. I see how you look at him, as though you want to devour him. Let him see that. Think about how you would go about seducing him."

Celeste looked at Phae, waiting for a response.

She realized the instructor had intuited everything Phae had been trying to hide. "I... I..." She lowered her eyes and then looked back up at Celeste. "Thank you."

As she walked back to join Finn, she thought about the beautiful and romantic night he had given her. She wanted to let him know that she was more than attracted to him. If there would ever be a man she wanted to make love with, it would be Finn.

She thought about Celeste's prompt, about how Phae would seduce Finn.

"What did she tell you? Are you okay?" Finn asked, giving her a questioning look.

"If I told you, then it wouldn't be a surprise." She winked at him and got into the dance pose.

The music started, and she stretched out her arms and waited until he walked toward her.

They practiced taking a side step and using their knees to make the hip movement more prominent. Phae got a case of the giggles. "I didn't know I could move my hips that much," she said.

"Shhh. You're going to get us in trouble if you keep giggling," Finn teased. She pinched her lips together to stop the laughter. "Besides, I like the way you move those hips." He gave her a purposefully rakish smile.

Phae was having fun. She felt like she was back in high school learning to dance for the prom, which she hadn't been able to attend. She had always liked dancing, but it was something she did when no one was around to see.

Celeste shouted that they needed to practice the steps as a pair. She went to each couple showing them the proper posture, gliding her hands along the men's shoulders and putting them on the men's hips to move them to the music. Phae's jaw dropped in surprise at the seductive movements.

The other women didn't seem to be bothered by the way Celeste touched their male partners, but it was getting on Phae's nerves.

Celeste came to the women next and showed them how they should stand and where they should put their arms. "Ladies! The next thing you need to learn is how to sway your body for your men."

Phae was beginning to dislike Celeste more and more. The knots in her stomach grew tighter, and her thermostat was overheating. When Celeste came over and snagged Finn to illustrate the next move Phae wanted to shout, *He's mine. Don't touch!* Her heartbeat increased as she tried to maintain her feminine façade and hide her killer instincts.

Phae's chest tightened further as she watched Celeste gyrate in front of Finn. Then she spun into him and put one of her legs up on his hip. Phae gulped. It looked so erotic.

Dropping her leg and stepping away, Celeste said, "He's all yours."

Phae didn't acknowledge Celeste's comment. She thought of Finn and told herself, *I can be seductive too, dammit.*

When she looked at him, he seemed distracted. She eventually realized he was still busy wondering what the surprise was. When he finally reached her, he put his hands on her waist. Her arms encircled his neck, and she laid her head on his chest for just a millisecond. Then she raised her head to look at him.

His eyes had a dreamy cast. She placed her hand on his chest and felt his rapid heartbeat. He laid his hand over hers. She smiled. "A penny for your thoughts."

"I think you already know." His voice was husky with a slight edge. His eyes shone with tenderness; there was nothing hard in his facial expression.

She felt safe and secure in Finn's arms and she rolled her head back, offering her neck to him. He pulled away, and she immediately felt deflated because he hadn't taken what she'd offered. It drove her to put more emphasis on the movements of her body. His steps were then bringing him closer to her. As he was ready to reach for her, she turned her back and danced away from him.

She suddenly understood the meaning of the dance; it was about conquering and losing.

She had taken a half step away from him when she felt him grab her hand and twirl her backward, this time into his arms so that her back arched. He wanted to be the conqueror.

She thought about her past life and how controlled she had felt. She would not let this conquest be so easy. She shoved Finn away from her and walked away, her steps fierce.

The blaze in his eyes stirred the latent passion inside her and made her want to convey to him how much she wanted him. Her heart beat rapidly as she thought about how far out of her comfort zone she was, and yet she was the most excited and alive.

With a deep breath, she closed her eyes and let the music engulf her. Finn had his hand outstretched for her to take, his one hip jutting out.

Her hand touched his, and he spun her around and under his arm. His fingertips at the base of her spine pushed her into him. When, after a few seconds, he pushed her out and away, she didn't resist. When it was time to return to him she walked back slowly… arching her back and with each step, accentuated slow hip and shoulder movements.

When she reached him, she stretched her arms up over her head, and slowly let the back of her hands shimmer down along her bust line. Then she turned her back to him.

He put his hands on her hips and drew her toward him. She could feel the movement of his hips and his hardness against her back. They swiveled in unison.

Phae imagined the soft, soulful voice of the Spanish singer pouring out words of love. The strumming of the guitar, the beat of maracas and bongo drums took her into an unknown world. Finn was parading her out away from him. She was very aware of everything about him and, when he spun her back in, he leaned to one side with his leg extended. He gently tugged her, inviting her to lean against his leg. All she could think was he made her feel sexy. Everything with Finn was magical.

The other instructor, Tony, came over and interrupted their dancing. He took hold of Phae's hand and twirled her around, dipping her so that his mouth was inches from her lips.

All she could think was, *Wow.*

With her head upside down, she glanced to Finn, whose scowl marred his handsome face. Initially, that expression made her feel anxious. Then she reminded herself how protective she'd felt when watching Celeste dance with Finn.

Tony gave Phae back to partner. "You two try it."

Phae understood what they were supposed to do. Excited by how quickly she had learned this dance, she gave Finn a look that communicated, "I'm ready if you are."

Their eyes locked. Finn stepped out, away from her, leaving her standing there alone. The only thing she could think to do was use her arms to motion to him. When he took her hand, he spun her into him, and in one movement, dipped her and kissed her. She was breathless and felt like she was floating.

Somewhere in the distance, she heard Tony's voice. "Ladies, let the man lead. Don't be afraid to let your body move to the music. Dancing is like making love. Let your partner know you love him."

Phae was dazed by the intensity of her reborn sexuality. She felt a soft, warm sensation around her heart that worked its way down to her womb and deeper, where she ached for release. She vibrated with joy and the life force flowing through her.

Their dance had urged her to push through the barriers of her fear and let go.

She also felt more than just desire and affection. The dance had brought out the sexuality she'd been hiding. It made her feel like a sexual siren. She found she liked the feeling.

The overwhelming fondness and craving sent a sweet, delicious wave down her body, unlike any she had experienced during her marriage. Before, she hadn't thought of herself as sexy or desirable. She'd thought perhaps she was as George had said—cold. She knew better now. A ball of need burst to life as they danced.

Phae still had doubts that she could trust her own judgment regarding love, men, and sexuality. After all, she had thought George was the right one. On the other hand, what she felt with Finn on the dance floor wasn't like anything she'd ever felt with George. With Finn, a power emanated from her own sexuality.

She'd never experienced such sexual magnetism with George, but, even so, she needed to keep her wits about her and think this through. She couldn't afford to let herself be carried away by emotions. She wanted more with Finn than she'd had with George.

She wanted to know the deeper side of Finn. She wanted to know what made him laugh, what made him sad, what he dreamed of. She wanted to share dreams and desires with him—something she had not done with anyone in a long time. What she wanted was a deeper connection, so that when their bodies became entangled, the pleasure would meld them together as hands explored and lips kissed from head to toe. Every time she looked at Finn, she felt heat throbbing in her core. Her heart danced with the same excitement that she now recognized made Finn want to touch her.

As the Rumba ended, she heard clapping and saw Tony, Celeste, and the other couples gathered around her and Finn. She straightened her posture.

"That was wonderful, you two," Tony and Celeste chimed.

Phae looked at Finn to see if he was as stunned as she was. Their breathing had slowed enough that Finn was able to speak. He smiled and said, "Thank you. Are you thirsty? I was going to get something to drink."

"Yes, that sounds fantastic. Soda will be all right."

"Celeste and Tony, would you like anything?"

They both declined and Finn excused himself to go for the drinks.

A few people came up to compliment Phae's dancing. When the crowd left, Celeste approached. "It is good to see him happy again." She gave Phae's hand a squeeze. "You are a lucky woman." She nodded in the direction Finn had gone. "That one is a good man. He will love you forever."

Celeste's words went to Phae's core; she felt like she'd had the air knocked out of her.

"You are wondering how I know?" Celeste smiled and shrugged. "He looks at you like he used to look at Angela."

Phae's heart tightened and yet overflowed with joy. She knew how much Finn had cared for Angela… she knew how devastated he had been when he lost her.

Phae lowered her eyes, humbled to be loved like that, even as she questioned whether she could love Finn as much in return. It scared and delighted her at the same time.

She felt Celeste waiting for her to say something.

"But we are not… dating. I'm his employee."

That sounded silly even to her ears. Tonight was a date. There was sexual tension between them. She hadn't fully realized until now that she wanted to be more than an employee.

She breathed a sigh of satisfaction, *it just happened*. Kisses here and there, holding hands when they walked, or sat at the kitchen table, talking. It had seemed so natural.

# Chapter Twenty-eight

It was one o'clock in the morning and they were nearing the hotel. Phae was giddy with excitement and happiness. She didn't know what to do with the energy running through her. She wanted to keep dancing, afraid it would all end if they didn't.

She walked backwards in front of Finn, teasing and taunting him to catch her. He laughed, but then he reached out and brought her to him. "I haven't had this much fun in a long time."

"Neither have I. Thank you." They started up the steps of the hotel. She was heady from the evening's events and from the acknowledgment that their relationship had changed from that of employee/employer to… friends. But it was more than friends?

They hadn't made love yet so weren't technically lovers. The thought excited her as she contemplated giving in to her desires. Phae stood on her tiptoes and kissed Finn. He broke away and stepped back. They both became quiet, and she wondered if Celeste had been wrong.

They entered the hotel lobby, and he pushed the button to summon the elevator. Once inside he pulled her close to him. She clung to his arm and rested her head on his shoulder.

When they arrived at the door to their suite, he stood there for a moment. "I feel like a teenager on my first date."

Phae laughed. "I know what you mean."

He unlocked the door and turned on the table lamp, which cast a glow over the room. Phae stood next to him and studied his face, wondering what he was thinking. Butterflies seemed to be growing in her stomach.

"You're quiet. Are you okay?"

She didn't want this night to end. She wanted to feel Finn's arms around her and to continue where they had left off earlier in the evening. "I'm just wondering how I am ever going to get to sleep after such an exciting night." She smiled at him as she walked across the room and opened the glass doors, wondering what she could do to postpone the end of the evening.

"Well, I'm going to start by taking a quick shower so my muscles don't stiffen up from all that dancing." He began to unbutton his shirt.

Phae felt her fingers tingle as she remembered playing with those buttons earlier. She held her breath, letting the memory of the foggy warmth of his kisses come crashing into her senses. Stalling, she walked over and turned off the light. The moonlight cast silhouettes on the wall.

These newfound desires took her out of her comfort zone, sending a dull ache through her body, making her long for a release.

She took a gulp. Heart pounding as she stuttered. "I have an idea. Why don't we use the hot tub to relax?"

She saw his forehead scrunch and his Adam's apple move. She held her breath, waiting for him to say something.

"I've never been in a hot tub before." She played with her bottom lip as she wondered whether she'd misread his signals. Silence prevailed until she wanted to scream, "Say something."

***

Finn wasn't sure he'd heard her correctly. They had been more amorous this evening than at any other time. He chalked it up to a romantic setting and wine. The attraction between them was delicate and needed protecting at all costs. She had been adamant about not wanting a relationship. He wondered if she was ready to take their relationship to a physically intimate level.

"Did you bring a bathing suit?" he asked, hoping her response would give him insight into whether she was ready to take their relationship in a more intimate direction.

She gave him a questioning look. "I thought my bra and panties could act as a swimsuit."

He grinned. "I like the way you think." As eager as he was, he didn't want to rush her.

Finn stripped down to his boxers and glanced over to see that Phae had removed her stockings and jewelry but was struggling with the zipper on her dress. "Here let me help you with that."

She bent her head forward and turned her back toward him. His fingers grazed over her creamy, soft skin, sending sparks through him. He let the palm of his hand slide over the long curve of her neck and brushed the sleeves from her slim, delicate shoulders. She turned around her arms clinging to her dress. He didn't try to hide the desire rising in him.

She let the silky fabric fall, revealing a lacy pink slip that hugged the swell of her breasts and cleavage. He took pleasure in letting his finger trace the line of pink lace that teased the upper curve of her breast.

The brush of her fingers was like feathers on his chest, setting off a chain reaction that led to heightened pleasure. He wanted their first time to be savored, to be delicious beyond words.

As they stood there, eyes locked, he moaned and took hold of her wrist. Her pulse hammered beneath his thumb. He knew if they stood there much longer, he would burst into a flame and take her and it would be done and gone as quick as it started.

Her hesitancy told him that this was new to her, and Finn wanted her to explore her sexuality. He wanted her to have fun, to wash away her fears of an intimate relationship. He kissed her temple as he whispered in her ear, "I'll meet you in the hot tub. I need to gather towels and grab us something to drink."

He was reluctant to let her go, but he wanted this to be perfect for her.

Phae turned and walked to the hot tub, stopping long enough to remove her slip. He quickly gathered the items and laid them on a table nearby. The partially hidden moon sent a halo of light over her serene face.

He ached with wanting, with need and passion. "You are an enchanting sight," he said, his voice husky.

They were sitting side by side in the hot tub so they could see each other. His fingers played with damp tendrils of hair that clung to her face. Her hardened nipples pebbled beneath her bra, and the dark circles of her areolas shadowed the wet fabric, enticing him.

He cupped her neck then lowered his lips to her mouth, kissing her deeply.

They were breathing heavily, her fingers raking through his hair. As much as he wanted to devour her in one swoop, he relished the tiny butterfly kisses she spread over his face and neck.

Gently, he slid her bra straps down and trailed kisses over the swell of her breasts, giving each globe tender caresses. She groaned with pleasure as his hands traveled down to stroke her belly. He was aware of her licking and circling his nipples with her tongue. He let his hand glide from her belly to her waist and up her back, reveling in skin soft as silk, until he felt an obstacle.

He unfastened her bra, releasing her breasts. He stroked his fingers over her soft breasts and teased her nipples. The sound of her soft mews drove him to lower his head. Her scent teased his nostrils as he bent to nibble and taste her nipples. Meanwhile her fingers roamed his stomach and slid into the waistband of his shorts.

He raised his head and their eyes met, reflecting each other's need and desire.

He trailed kisses along her shoulder and face. Her intake of air continued as his fingers played with her nipples, arousing her more. He trailed kisses up one side of her neck to her face. He lingered at her lips, to tease and nibble, moving down the other side behind her ear where her rose fragrance tickled his nose.

Her mews of delight and the way she moved her head to give him clear access drove him on, and he kissed the swell of her breast. He heard her sighs turn to soft pants as he continued to play there, teasing soft, creamy skin. Her eyes held a dreamy look as she pressed herself against him.

Her hands roamed along his firm thighs now, but hesitated as they neared his hard rod. He longed to have her stroke him. His heart thumped with anticipation as he waited for her to take hold of him. "Go ahead, touch me, show me what you want."

He trailed kisses from behind her ear to the hollow between her breasts. When she made no move to touch him, he took her hand and placed it on his shaft. He heard her little gasp and then felt the soft skin of her hand as she wrapped it firmly around him. She sank against him, and he kissed her deeply, as her hand began to stroke him through his boxers.

He broke the kiss, his eyes never leaving hers, as he removed his shorts. Her hand returned to her ministrations.

He felt himself twitch as though his shaft were a lightning rod searching for its target. He let out a moan of pleasure. He wanted more. He wanted to be inside her.

"I want you, Finn." Her voice was filled with desire.

He pulled her to him, and staring deep into her eyes, lifted her onto his lap.

She was panting and writhing with need, her warm heat moving against his hard member. He stroked the edge of lace on the leg of her panties, each caress taking him closer and closer to her molten center. Finally, when he could wait no more, he cupped her mound.

He saw her wince and pull back. "Did I hurt you?"

"No. I have a cramp in my leg." Her voice strained, and her forehead creased. "I'm sorry…"

He thought for a moment she wanted to stop. He would've been immensely disappointed.

"Tell me where it hurts." He saw a mixture of pain and worry on her face. "I'll massage it and see if we can make it feel better."

She bit her bottom lip. "It's my hip." She twisted and rubbed her side. He lifted her and sat her back down on the seat of the tub, letting her head rest in one arm, while his other arm rubbed the creak out of her hip.

He felt her relax, and he gradually lightened the pressure he was applying to her hip.

They sat there enjoying the music of the tub jets and twinkling stars. "Do you want to go inside?" he asked.

He saw her frown. Her bright eyes clouded over with disappointment. It dawned on him that she thought he'd lost interest in her.

He lifted her chin and gave her a light kiss. "Phae, I want you. I thought it might be more comfortable if we went inside... on the bed."

He felt the nod of her head against his chest. Then she sat up. He reached behind him for a towel and stood to wrap it around his hips. He gently hung a towel over her shoulders.

They walked arm and arm into the bedroom. Finn grabbed an extra towel and began drying her hair. Afterward, she took the towel from him and wiped his arms, back, and chest.

When she was finished, he reclaimed the towel and knelt to dry her feet and legs. He picked up one leg to dry her foot and his eyes traveled from her dainty toes up her leg, to her knee, and beyond to her lush thighs and hips. His eyes lingered on the panties covering the area he desired the most.

He patted and dried all the way up. He started on the other leg. Slowly he took his time, sometimes letting his fingers caress her thigh. He wondered how she'd taste and how his cock would feel when he was inside her. She played with his hair and each time his fingers went closer to her core she whispered, "Please."

Phee opened her legs a little wider, tempting him with desire and release. Her whispers spurred him to pat and rub her panties with the towel, lingering and applying pressure to her mound. She pushed herself closer.

"May I remove the panties?" he asked.

She nodded.

His fingers gently slid inside the lacy waistband. He nudged the material down two inches. He let his tongue graze her lower stomach. She cried out. He moved the elegant fabric down to expose her femininity. He cupped her buttocks and drove her into his face. He could smell her unique scent.

He felt her stomach clench as if she were holding back. He slid the panties the rest of the way off. He kissed her thighs and let his tongue explore the groove where her leg joined her body. She moaned, and he heard her whisper, "That feels wonderful."

Her words urged him on. He slid his hand between her legs and his thumb rubbed the top her mound, his fingertips teasing her opening. He could feel her dampness.

"Oh, Finn, please. You're driving me crazy." She lifted, arching toward him.

He was delighted with her reaction to his touches. He could feel the desire warming his stomach as he anticipated the ecstasy awaiting him. He wanted to hear her beg him not to stop.

He inserted one finger and heard her gasp of pleasure as he drove a second finger into her core.

"Deeper, Finn." The huskiness of her voice made him withdraw slightly and then go deeper.

Her muscles tightened around his fingers. He teased and probed. The towel around his hips had fallen off, and he wanted to feel her hands on him again, but more than that, he wanted to feel her muscles tighten around his cock. He wanted to feel her release.

He sucked in air, feeling like he was going to explode any second. He cupped her face, and their eyes met, her eyes glazed with passion.

He took several steps backward until he could feel the bed behind his legs. Finn kissed her and slowly laid her on the bed, following her down onto the soft surface. His cock nestled between her legs, but he didn't want to take her yet. He wanted more exploration.

He kissed her face, temples, and lips. "Tell me what you want, Phae." He searched her face for some answer, and when none came, he slid the tip of his cock into her opening. "Is this what you want?" He saw her hands clutch the bed covering.

"Ohh yes, Finn, yes."

"I'd rather caress your body, kiss you from head to toe running my tongue along every delightful inch of you." He flicked his tongue on her nipples.

"Ohhh, please," she cried.

"Please what, Phae?" He felt her wiggling and arching her back to get closer to his cock.

She reached down between them. "I want you inside me. I've never wanted anything so badly before."

His hands moved to cup her butt and pushed into her a little further.

"I can't wait, Finn. Don't torture me anymore."

He didn't say anything.

She smiled a wicked sultry smile. "Have your way with me. I trust you."

Watching her face, he saw the desire she felt and the trust she placed in him, and he knelt and gently licked the folds of her sex. She closed her eyes on a moan when he slipped his tongue inside her.

Her long slender fingers raked through his hair and her body arched, asking him for more. He gave her what she wanted, stroking deeper with each thrust of his tongue. She met him at every thrust, and he could feel her release building, but he pulled away before she could come.

Her eyes were wide and wild with desire as she crashed into his chest like a freight train and made him ache with the need to be inside her. But even more than he wanted to be inside her, he wanted to hear her tell him where to touch her.

When she arched her back and groaned he heard her whispered plea. "Don't stop."

He thrust his tongue and flicked her clit and then went deeper.

"Finn," she gasped for air, shaking her head.

She seemed to be out of control with desire. Her nub was swollen. There was a passion inside her equal to his own. This was about giving her a memory that would soothe her far into the future. Hopefully, a future they would spend together.

His gut clenched tight, his reserve of willpower quickly dwindling. Her gasp slid along his senses as she dug into his back. When he spread her lips wider and sucked, she cried out. Quick pulses and the release of thick creamy juices and a long, drawn out moan of pleasure escaped her. Her loss of control was unbelievable. Unexpected. He welled with emotion at her release. He wanted to give her more, to be inside her the next time to feel her orgasm.

He massaged her stomach and planted kisses on her belly, letting her catch her breath, letting her revel in the pleasure.

She put her forehead on his. "I can't believe how wonderful that felt. Thank you." She kissed him. "What about you Finn? You don't want me to take care of you? Is that why you didn't… stop?"

He rolled her back under him. Her forehead was creased and little frown lines showed around her eyes. "I want you more than anything. I didn't stop because I enjoyed watching you."

She bit her bottom lip, and the sparkle returned to her eyes. "Really?"

"Yes, really." He kissed her lightly. "But we're not done yet. I want to pleasure you over and over."

She started to speak, but her voice was muffled. "I want to give you pleasure, too."

"Hmm, I'm all yours." He lay back with his hands behind his head.

She moved down his legs with a soft, gentle massaging motion. When she came to his heat, she stroked him. His heart thundered in his chest at her sweet, soft touches. Her fingers slid down the outside of his thighs and back up his inner thigh, teasing a trail inches from his balls. She tormented him with her fingers, and her tongue caressed him everywhere, but where he really wanted to feel her hands, her mouth, her inner heat.

The anticipation made him ache and caused his member to strain toward her as she skimmed down his legs and back up. He wanted her… needed to be closer, needed her to touch him.

He didn't want to rush her as she seemed to be enjoying tantalizing him. He knew the pleasure one derived from giving pleasure to another.

"Do you like that?" she asked, her voice hesitant and soft.

"Mmm. It's heaven. Don't stop."

He kept his eyes closed, wanting to savor every touch.

She kissed him gently on the lips and began to trail kisses down his chest to his torso. His stomach tautened with hope she would put her delicious mouth on his rod. Before he finished that thought, he felt her thumb caress the tip of his penis. Then her tongue flicked over it, and she glided her tongue up and down his length. His entire body throbbed with longing.

He knotted his hands in the bedclothes, desperate to be inside her, wanting them to experience release at the same time. He imagined them teasing and kissing each other, her soft, warm body beneath him, but his need for her was driving him out of control.

He groaned. He couldn't wait any longer. He pulled her up and kissed her. "Please, Phae, I want to be inside you now." His voice sounded strangled even to his own ears.

"I want you, too."

"I can't wait any longer." In one swift movement, he rolled her over and let the tip of his cock enter her. She spread her legs wider to welcome him. He pulled back out and rubbed against her sex, moving up and down but depriving her of all of him.

"Why are you teasing me?" She nipped his shoulder.

He raised himself on his arms so he could look at her… and enjoy her reaction. "I want to see your face as I arouse you."

She reached behind his neck, pulling him closer. She wet her lips with the tip of her tongue. Desire shone in her eyes, making him want her all the more.

He looked down at her to watch her facial expression as he entered her completely.

Pleasure flowed over her features when he slid his erection into her. They moved in harmony with each thrust, creating a deeper sense of urgency. Faster and harder he thrust until he felt her muscles tighten around his cock, making it harder to move in and out. He was losing the last vestiges of control. He quivered with the need for release. Her eyes were wide and begging him to give her satisfaction. "Now, my sweet Phae, now."

Lust was tearing through him, adrenaline spiking and they both came.

***

Phae felt his release explode inside her, each pulse giving her more pleasure. She didn't want him to move. It was as if she was floating down from the sky, with a shower of glittering stars around her. She was filled with an overwhelming sense of bliss.

He kissed her face. "You're beautiful."

She gave him a smile. "You make me feel beautiful."

He rolled to his side, taking her with him. Her head rested on his chest, and she ran her fingers along his stomach, drawing little circles.

"You're trembling. What are you thinking about, Phae?" He pulled the blanket up around her and kissed her forehead.

Every fiber of her body was tingly and soft. She had never felt so soft before. She had let herself give in to the pleasure he aroused in her, and it was as though he had awakened her from her lonely captivity.

"Hmm. I'm thinking how wonderful I feel and what a fantastic lover you are." She shifted closer to him and let her hands play with the hair on the nape of his neck. "I'm also sleepy."

# Chapter Twenty-nine

Phae slowly opened her eyes to see Finn's head propped up with his hand as he looked down at her. She smiled and touched his face, and he kissed her forehead.

"You were remarkable last night," he whispered. "Thank you."

"You liked my dancing, did you?" she asked in a light, airy voice.

He laughed. She liked the sound of his baritone laughter.

"We tripped the light fantastic, but it wasn't the dancing. Your moves were delightful, but it's the hot tub that set me on fire."

Embarrassment flooded through her when she remembered her wanton behavior. She shook it off, letting her fingers walk on his chest. "I don't know what got into me. You seem to bring out… this other side of me that I'm not familiar with." She lowered her eyes to hide her embarrassment.

George hadn't liked it when she'd tried to spice up their lovemaking. He'd asked her where she learned this or that. Then he'd told her it wasn't becoming of a wife and was more the action of a harlot. Funny, she hadn't ever thought of it until now, but she should've asked him how he knew the actions of a harlot.

Finn reached for her hand. "Do you regret it?"

She lifted her head from his chest to look at him. "No. Not at all. It's just that… this isn't the place to talk about it."

He pulled back to look at her. "Phae, we can talk anywhere. I like talking here. It's better than sex." He gave her a mischievous smile. "There's nothing between us, not even clothing. We're naked and vulnerable, which leads to discussion that is more honest. So spill, woman."

She liked the way he called her "woman." It made her feel sensuous and loved. The thought of being loved no longer scared her. She realized that she had been falling in love with Finn a little bit more as each day had passed and as they had gotten to know each other better.

"You make me laugh," she began. "You're so light-hearted and fun. I've not ever experienced that before." She fidgeted with her hands. "I don't want to talk about George when I'm in your bed."

"Our bed," he corrected her.

She smiled at that, liking the way it sounded. "I want our bed to be happiness and fun, not serious discussion."

He pushed his knee between her legs. "Well, technically this isn't our bed, it's the hotel's bed. Does that make it better?" he asked with a smirk.

Finn pulled her closer and pinched her bottom. "I can think of other things we can do."

"Give me a moment to use the bathroom," she said, then realized that it had been dark the previous night when they'd made love, and that if she got out of bed to go to the bathroom, he'd see her boobs drooping to her belly button. She grabbed the towel on the floor to cover herself.

When she stepped out of the bathroom, she found he had switched places on the bed. He lifted the covers, his eyes dark and dreamy. "Drop the towel. I want to see all of you."

She did as he asked but practically dove into the bed and under the covers next to him. She wasn't used to parading around naked in front of a man. It felt awkward, but when he wrapped his arms around her, it made her feel like a goddess. His caresses aroused her, and his whispered words about what he was going to do to her made her forget everything but him and the pleasure they gave one another.

Once more they made slow, passionate love. After they had finished and were lying facing each other, he took hold of her hand and stared at their entwined fingers.

The suite's doorbell rang and startled her. Her body stiffened, and her heart pounded at the thought of anyone discovering they had shared a bed.

"That must be room service. I ordered breakfast for us."

Finn got out of bed and put his pajama bottoms on. She watched him leave the bedroom and then got up and put on her robe. When she heard the close of the front door, she went out into living area.

"The coffee smells delicious."

He poured her a cup and handed it to her. She took it and looked at him. "I could get used to this."

Finn reclaimed the cup from her and placed it on the table. He wrapped his arms around her waist and nibbled on her neck. "And I could get used to this."

He eventually released her and handed her coffee back to her. "Eat some breakfast. What would you like for us to do today?"

"I thought you had meetings."

"Yes, this morning. However, we will have all afternoon and evening together."

She leaned across the table and kissed him. "Anything. Surprise me." She tilted her head. "I've never been to Rome before. Everything is new and exciting to me."

They ate and talked over breakfast. He left her to go shower and dress. She sat on the balcony staring out at the sea and letting the warm memories of their lovemaking wash over her.

***

Finn studied Phae. She sat with a look of bliss on her face. "Do I get a kiss goodbye?" he asked from behind her.

She rose and stepped into his arms, kissing him lightly. Her hair was still tousled, and her robe had a gap that revealed her creamy skin and supple breasts.

He pulled her to him, and his lips crushed down on hers. He tilted her back, and she clung to him as though she were falling off a cliff. She opened her mouth, and he took the opportunity to play havoc on her tongue.

Finally he broke the kiss and straightened. He could tell she was reeling and unsteady. "That's so you don't forget about me while I'm gone," he teased. He followed with a kiss on the forehead. "I'll be back at noon."

***

Once he'd gone, Phae flopped down into the chair. For several surprised seconds, she sat there feeling like a balloon with a leak until her mind slowly returned to reality.

Everything was too perfect. He had awakened, accepted and encouraged her sensuality. Finn treated her with tenderness and respect. She felt tears gathering in her eyes as the reality of the situation settled in. She was in love with Finn. It felt wonderful to have this connection with him. It overwhelmed her that he accepted her for who she was. She felt nurtured… and worshiped. Something she had never experienced before. She realized now what had been missing from her marriage.

Phae's mind whirled with questions. How would her children react to her having a relationship with a man other than their father? Did she love Finn enough to take the risk, to jump over the hurdles? Would she be able to stand up to her children if they didn't approve? And if it came down to a choice between her children and Finn, which would she choose?

Her grandchildren, with their sweet, adorable faces, flashed through her mind. She would be heartbroken if Kera and Jeffrey refused to let her see them. Phae's hands covered her heart. It was like an elephant was sitting on her chest as she considered the question.

She rubbed her arms and tightly shut her eyes, allowing several cleansing breaths to clear her mind. She fretted over how many people would get hurt. All she could envision was that no matter what she chose, people were going to get hurt. Including her.

She shook her head to dislodge the dark thoughts.

A picture formed in her mind of large family gatherings with her children and Izzy's family, only she saw Jeff and Kera sulking. She just wanted everyone to be happy; that would complete her happiness. She needed to think positive. Maybe she was worrying for nothing. Of course her children would be happy for her.

That prompted questions of where she and Finn would live. Close to her children or close to Izzy and Luke? What if Finn didn't want to get married; would she be able to accept living together?

She had lost track of how long she had sat there. She heard church bells in the distance indicating it was ten in the morning. Rousing herself, she decided she had better get a move on. Finn would be back in less than two hours. The thought of his return put a smile on her face. She felt giddy with excitement. Together they could work out the issues about where to live.

She rose from the chair feeling young and alive and danced her way into her bedroom to shower and dress.

Phae wasn't sure what Finn would plan for the day, so she opted to wear a cotton floral skirt and a white blouse that crossed and tied in the front. She was in the living room just before noon when she heard the elevator ping. She hurried to the door and opened it to find Finn with a bouquet of flowers, a wicked gleam in his eye.

She was surprised at how much she had missed him and went into his arms to give him a kiss. He gave her a little grunt.

"What's the matter?" she asked.

"You're all dressed and ready to go. I was hoping for a little afternoon delight."

Her arms were around his waist, and she slowly let her hands roam to his buttocks. "That can be arranged," she said. A floating sensation enveloped her and a throbbing, warm heat spread through her.

Finn's lips formed an equally wicked grin. "These are for you," he said handing her the flowers.

As she took the bouquet and sniffed them, Finn found and undid the tie on her blouse. He pulled a red rose from among the cluster and trailed it along the lacy edge of her bra.

"I love roses."

He tapped her nose the petals. "Then follow me, my little flower."

They entered their bedroom, removing clothing, their hunger for each other needing to be sated.

Later, they were lying in bed in the afterglow of their lovemaking. "I see the benefits of afternoon naps. We'll need to add this to our daily routine."

Phae lifted her head to look at him. "What are you suggesting?"

Before he could answer, Finn's cell phone rang. He picked it up and looked at it. "It's Izzy," he said.

# Chapter Thirty

"Hi, sweetheart. Is everything okay?"

Finn could barely hear his daughter's response. "Izzy, speak up. Why are you whispering?" He glanced over at Phae. She had tilted her head and was giving him a questioning look.

"I can't talk, Dad, I have people here. Is Phae with you?"

Finn pulled Phae closer to him. "Yes, she's here." He noticed her look of concern.

"Put me on speakerphone." Finn looked at Phae and shrugged. "She wants to talk to both of us." He pushed the button.

"Hi, Izzy is everything okay?"

"Phae, your children are here."

Finn saw the color drain from Phae's face. Her forehead crinkled, but he couldn't tell if it was in confusion or concern. He squeezed her in a gesture of support.

"When did they arrive?" Phae asked.

Her eyes roamed the room looking everywhere but at him. Her chin quivered as she swallowed hard and he thought for a moment she was going to cry. He thought of how soft and relaxed she had been moments earlier. Now her body stiffened as she edged away from him.

"About thirty minutes ago. I explained that you and Dad were in Rome and due back tomorrow." The silence seemed to go on forever. "Phae… your son didn't seem at all happy about that."

183

Finn noticed her breathing had become quick and shallow. Something that resembled panic had darkened her beautiful hazel eyes, and she bit her bottom lip.

"Izzy, are you all right?" he asked.

"Yes, Dad, I'm fine. I came into the kitchen to make us some lunch and to call you."

"We'll be there as soon as we can."

After they disconnected the call, Phae lay in his arms very still. He thought her reaction to her children's visit odd. He thought it equally odd that they had showed up with no notice. Perhaps it was that which seemed to distress her more.

"What's troubling you? Aren't you happy about your children visiting?"

"I don't want to discuss it now." She threw back the covers. "I need to pack."

He felt a tug at his heart, a strange combination of being miffed that she was practically running from him and was dismissing him at the same time.

Finn released her. Phae got out of bed and looked around the room as if she didn't know what to do next. He picked up his phone and called his pilot. As he walked to the bathroom, he stopped and looked back at her, piercing her with his eyes. "Just get dressed and don't worry about doing anything else," he commanded. "I will contact the concierge and ask him to have everything packed and sent to Mallorca. The car is waiting for us outside. We can be in the air shortly and… home in a few hours."

It was a tight fit in the chopper, but he didn't mind. He grabbed Phae's hand, and her eyes lifted to his.

"Thank you for everything," she mouthed. Then she became withdrawn and quiet.

The sinking feeling in his stomach wouldn't ease up. To think, just earlier they had been in the throes of love and passion. He'd been wondering about proposing to her that evening. Now she was behaving as if she'd received news of a death, or as if the world were coming to an end.

Finn started to wonder whether, if she was forced to make a choice, if she would choose him.

He also wondered what hold Kera and Jeff had over her that their visit had caused such a change.

They didn't speak much on the way home. Riding in the helicopter felt more like riding in a hearse. The drive up the mountain was no different. He didn't know what to say to her, and he was afraid he wouldn't like the answers to his questions if he asked them.

By the time they arrived back at the villa, nightfall was on the horizon. Clouds accumulated and the wind had picked up. The weather matched his tumultuous mood.

They walked toward the front door. Phae reached out and took his hand. Finn could feel the tremor in her touch. He didn't like this tension between them. Whatever else was going on, if there was going to be a future for the two of them, they needed to be on the same page.

He stopped and drew her close. He wanted to savor this moment, uncertain what was going to happen or who she would ultimately choose.

"Please don't be angry with me."

He closed his eyes and squeezed her a bit tighter, then he lifted her chin so he could look into her eyes. He was dreading what waited for them on the other side of the door.

"It's silly, but I feel like a teenager about to be told by her parents that they don't approve of her boyfriend." Phae blinked.

He gave her a questioning look. "I'm not angry with you, Phae. I'm worried and don't understand why it's so important to please them."

She looked up, her face etched with sorrow. "My entire life has been about pleasing my family. Jeffrey is a lot like his father. He's not going to be happy. But Kera, I'm not sure. She does whatever Jeffrey tells her."

Frustration and confusion flashed through Finn. "Why do you need their approval to live your life, Phae?"

***

Phae was startled by Finn's question. He'd forced her into considering the one thing that led to a sense of clarity. "It's not as much a matter of needing their approval as it is that I don't like conflict."

She hung her head. She knew in her mind that none of this was fair to Finn. He deserved more, and she wanted to give it to him, but she was worried about losing confidence when she faced her children.

As they stepped through the door, Finn said, "Remind me to get a hot tub."

That snapped the tension and Phae giggled. Finn kissed her. He was good for her… he knew how to make her laugh.

# Chapter Thirty-one

"Mother! What are you doing?"

Phae jumped back at the sound of Jeffrey's raised voice. She was shocked to see him standing in front of her, outrage apparent in every line of his body.

"Is this what you came to Spain for? To gallivant around with a man?"

Phae's stomach dropped. She shivered at the hostile, demeaning tone in her son's voice. Mortified at his words, she glanced at Finn, feeling ashamed and embarrassed.

He squeezed her hand and a sense of connection passed between them.

Phae had learned long ago not to show fear when facing Jeffrey. She straightened her spine. "Jeff and Kera, what a pleasant surprise. I'm sorry I wasn't here when you arrived. Had I known you were coming I would have stayed behind."

"Don't pretend you don't notice I'm angry."

A spark of rebellion, or was it courage to fight for what she wanted, ignited within her. Finn's words rang in her ears. He was right… her children were no longer babies relying on her for support. They were adults in their own right. She hadn't realized until now how much her son sounded like his father—like an outraged spouse, but Jeffrey was her son, not her husband.

Phae looked at him sideways. "You're angry, why is that?"

Their eyes locked. Phae refused to surrender.

"I… I guess it's none of my business what you do, Mother."

Phae tried to remain expressionless. A feeling of power that she had not kowtowed to Jeffrey's anger shot through her. She glanced quickly at Finn. His look made her stand a little taller, and it filled her with strength. She was not going to let her son manipulate her into feeling guilty.

She put her hands in her pockets to hide the shakiness.

Jeffrey turned his back on her. "Our father, your husband, is probably rolling in his grave at your scandalous behavior." His back was rigid, his posture stiff, as if he was going to march into war, and his voice dripped with unsweetened honey, thick yet sour.

Jeffrey's words fueled Phae's anger. How dare he bring up his father rolling in his grave! She was also saddened that George's attitude had carried down to their child.

Phae pursed her lips. "What is so scandalous? After fifteen years of being a widow, I'm not allowed to have a life?"

Jeffrey's mouth opened as if he were about to say something and then closed.

"I'm your mother. I don't need to ask your permission for anything that I do, and I shouldn't need to remind you that you are a guest in this house."

Phae inhaled. She continued calmly but with a slight edge to her voice. "Jeff and Kera, I would like you to meet Finn Callahan, my boss and Izzy's father. I assume you've introduced yourselves."

Finn extended his hand, but Jeffrey ignored it. "Your mother has spoken fondly of both of you." Kera hesitantly shook Finn's hand.

Kera turned and embraced her mother. "I'm happy to see you, Mom. I've missed you."

"Thank you, dear. I've missed you too!"

Phae heard a grunt from Jeffrey, and he mumbled something under his breath.

George had always muttered under his breath and, listening to her son do the same thing, it grated on Phae. She had a lot to say as well. The desire to get this out in the open and be done with it exploded within her. "Do you have something to say, Jeffrey?" she challenged.

The butterflies in her stomach multiplied, but she was tired of being manipulated.

Jeffrey straightened to his full height of six feet and planted himself as if he were on a basketball court anticipating being charged. "Yes, I do." The look he gave her was filled with disdain. "Dad warned us you might go off on a whirlwind." His tone was accusatory but filled with pride that his father's prediction had come to fruition. "I never expected you to find another man." He looked at her with disgust.

For the first time in her life, Phae had the urge to slap the smug expression off his face.

"Especially since father was understanding of your coldness toward him."

The unfairness of the accusation was like a stiff uppercut to the chin that left her seeing stars. Phae's heart pounded. She could not believe what she had just heard. Her stomach twisted into knots and pain radiated in her chest. His words stung. She wanted to stomp her foot at the unfairness. At his blindness. At his utter stupidity.

Instead, she said, "Stop. That's enough. I will not tolerate this disrespectful behavior from you. Nor will I discuss my marriage with you, especially when you only have half a story." With shaky hands and legs, she took a few steps toward Jeffrey. "That's partly my fault. I've been quiet far too long."

She sucked in air and swallowed. "I've been the outsider in this family since before you were able to walk. I protected you from the truth and let your father's vision of reality dominate." She drew another deep breath and let it out, a sense of resolve filling her. "No more. It ends here. Today."

Phae looked to Finn and Izzy. "I'm sorry you all have to hear this." She glanced at Kera and noticed that her daughter's shoulders were slumped. Phae had mixed emotions there. On one hand, she was angry with Kera for going to her brother to tattle that she was in Italy with a man, but she also felt sorry for her daughter.

No matter what she felt about Kera's role in this fiasco, Phae wanted to de-escalate things with Jeffrey by removing herself from the venom of Jeffrey's presence just as she had done with George. She needed to flee the conflict, but running away was what she had always done. Always being the one to back down had only allowed George's version of events to dictate. She couldn't afford to do that anymore. Not when her life and happiness depended on it.

"Have you ever considered the possibility that coldness was what your father liked?" She waited.

Jeffrey shrugged.

"Every marriage takes two to make it or break it. He wasn't exactly innocent."

"Don't try to make Dad look like the bad guy. You're the one shacked up with another man!" He spat the words as if they were dirty, vile.

"Jeffrey. Maybe we should hear Mom out." Kera's tone was patronizing and suspicious. But there was also an element of tentativeness as if she was afraid her brother would turn his venom on her.

Jeffrey looked at Kera with poison in his little black eyes. His face twisted with fury as he clenched his fists.

Phae wondered if Kera had been as afraid to stand up to her brother as she had been to stand up to George. After all, Kera had seemed genuinely pleased to see her.

Jeffrey finally gave Kera a quick, cunning smile. "Okay, we'll listen to her lies." He rested against the doorframe, legs and arms crossed. George had taken that same smug, condescending stance. He'd made Phae feel small… insignificant… like a child who had to explain in detail their whereabouts. "It might be good for him…" Jeffrey nodded his head in Finn's direction, "to hear what kind of woman our mother is."

Those words made their torturous way to Phae's soul. She expected to see drops of blood on the carpet from her broken heart, but the heat of her anger was enough to cauterize the wound.

Phae felt Finn's physical strength as he came and stood behind her, his hands resting on her shoulders, offering support. In a voice that could chill to the bone marrow, Finn said, "You are treading on thin ice. I will not allow anyone to disrespect a woman, let alone a mother, as you are disrespecting yours."

Phae reached for Finn's arm. She was trembling. "Finn, please."

"I will not allow anyone to hurt you."

She was surprised at the softness and the strength in Finn's tone when he spoke to her compared to the coldness in his gaze when his eyes darted to Jeffrey. "I would be happy to take this outside."

"He is angry at me." She bit her lip. "We need to have this out once and for all."

Finn's eyes were alight with something like fury as his gaze rested on Jeffrey. "I'm not moving from this spot, Phae."

In the past, Phae had avoided conflict at all costs. Having someone defend her was new to her, but she had to confront this on her own. Finn meant well, and it felt good to have someone care enough to rise to her defense, but it worried her too. She didn't want anyone to get hurt because of her. She didn't want that responsibility… or that guilt.

Phae ignored Finn's anger; the last thing she wanted was to either argue with Finn or encourage him. Instead, she turned her attention to her children as she tried to avert a disaster.

Phae looked at each of them in turn. "I've protected you for too long." She paused to collect herself. "Your father was a verbally, mentally and emotionally abusive man. It started shortly after we were married. Then when you kids were born, it got worse. At first, I thought it was jealousy because I gave my attention to you." Phae rubbed her hands together, feeling suddenly cold while she remembered the emotional trauma she'd suffered at George's hands. "Then he started becoming manipulative. If I didn't do what he wanted, he would grab you kids and put you in the car and not tell me where he was taking you."

She gulped, and her throat felt dry.

"When I would make plans for a family outing, he would tell me to stay home. He didn't want me with you. If I insisted, he would call me names and say I was incompetent to care for you." Phae eyed Kera warily. Kera had that deer caught in headlights look. "Kera, you would cry because you wanted to go. Rather than disappoint you, I would stay home."

Tears welled in her own eyes as the age-old layers of those memories, the reminders of loneliness and being unloved, whirled to life. "It was his decision to sleep in another room, not mine. I saw no need to share that information with you. You were children."

Phae took refuge in the silence that followed, collecting her thoughts and waiting for a response.

She looked over at Jeffrey, who had moved from the wall and taken a seat on the sofa. He leaned forward with his arms between his legs and his fingers forming a steeple. "I don't remember it that way." His tone was caustic. "I remember you turning your back on us and telling us to go." His eyes were full of resentment. He jerked up from the sofa, with an angry, menacing glare. "You stayed home and left us to deal with his temper. You didn't care what happened to us. Even Dad said so."

Phae felt a dull rumbling in her gut. A painful flash entered her mind as she recalled those times when she'd wanted to take the children to the zoo or on a trip. George would become excessively uptight. It was as if he couldn't deal with a change to his environment. It was only later, after his death, that she'd learned that a change of routine was frightening for a person with obsessive-compulsive disorder because they felt out of control.

"Jeffrey, I did care. I thought walking away and letting your dad take charge was the best thing." She massaged her forehead. She debated with herself whether to tell them about the mental illness.

"I've learned since then that he had OCD that I didn't know how to handle."

"A mental illness," Jeffrey scoffed. "You're a real piece of work, Mom!" Their eyes met and locked. "What a vile thing to say about someone who isn't here to defend himself."

Phae wanted to sink to the floor. Finn's grasp on her shoulders tightened. She rolled her head back and closed her eyes. "Dear God, help me," she whispered. If she thought the pain and hurt George had inflicted was awful, this from her son was ten times worse.

She lowered her head to her chest. Perhaps she shouldn't have said anything. But they did need to know, since it probably was genetic.

Slowly she raised her head and looked from Jeffrey to Kera. "You're right. Maybe I shouldn't have said it. But I'm not going to apologize for the truth."

Phae softened her tone. "You said I left you to deal with his anger. You're telling me he was allowed to be angry, but I wasn't." She paused. The words spoken aloud made her ask, "Why are you so angry with me?"

Phae could hear the clock ticking and felt the breeze from the sea as it wound its way into the room.

She saw Jeffrey's head bob slightly. Then he raised his eyes. "Because I grew to hate him," he spat out. "It was as if you knew making plans to go somewhere would set him off. Then you'd stay home alone, and we'd have to go with him."

Phae's hand flew to her mouth. She was stunned at this revelation. She'd wanted them all to have adventures, to see things, to have fun. The room was spinning. She hadn't forced them to go with George.

Phae sagged against Finn. He whispered in her ear, "Do you want to sit down?"

Phae shook her head. Her throat felt constricted.

Kera walked over to where Jeffrey stood and clung to his arm.

Her son launched in again. "Kera would cry because she wanted you. Dad would slap her and tell her to stop crying, or he'd give her something to cry about."

Phae was horrified. She searched her memories trying to make sense of it. The children had come home and gone directly to their rooms. When she had asked how the outing had been, eager for details of the adventures she hadn't been able to participate in, they had given her short, clipped answers. She had assumed they were angry with her for not going. When she had questioned George, he had indicated that the kids were tired and upset that she'd chosen to stay behind because they thought she didn't want to be with them.

Phae's heart ached at the memory of those days. Looking back, she recalled that sly smile he'd given her when he said, *"Of course I told them that wasn't true."* Now she wondered if he'd been lying to her all those times.

"When I tried to calm Kera, he told me to stop being a wimp and to leave her alone. Do you have any idea what it's like to be unable to comfort your baby sister? It made me feel like a coward."

Phae took a deep, pained breath and closed her eyes. Guilt consumed her. She shook her head. "I am so sorry. I didn't know any of this was going on. When you kids became teenagers, you had your own activities. I didn't bother to create family events anymore. I… was happy to have time with you alone as I drove you to your various activities."

"Thank God you came to your senses." This time it was Kera who spoke up. "We worried that you were going to make Dad take us. We didn't want him there to criticize us or call us names in front of our friends."

Phae put her face in her hands. "I don't know what to say, except I'm sorry. I was young and ill-prepared to handle a man like your father. He was a hard worker, and I made excuses for his behavior, telling myself he was tired."

Phae's chin began to tremble, and she felt as if she was breaking apart inside. All she could think about was how blind she had been and how she had allowed all this to come about. She wondered if they'd get past it.

She opened her mouth to speak, but no words were formed.

Eventually she said, "It's not an excuse, but I didn't know." She paused, and it occurred to her that some of Jeffrey's anger had now dissipated.

"Tracy left me," he admitted. "She said that I was mean and controlling." He lowered his gaze. "Why didn't you leave Dad?"

Phae saw the look of hurt and self-derision on Jeffrey's face. She had talked to him about his anger issues. She realized now, and probably Jeffrey did too, that he had learned these traits from George.

Phae looked at Kera. For the first time, she saw that her daughter was timid and quiet, letting Jeffrey do all the talking. She had probably learned that the best way to avoid getting hurt physically or mentally was to keep quiet.

George had pitted the children against each other, just as he had pitted the children against her. They were all victims of George's illness. She wished she had known and consulted with someone sooner.

Clearing her throat, she said, "There were lots of reasons I couldn't leave. How was I going to take care of you children? I had no money, no job skills. I tried to leave him once. He became so despondent that I feared he might hurt himself. I… couldn't be responsible for that. Believe it or not, I did care for him in my own way. I thought I could help him. But he didn't think he needed any help."

Phae turned slightly to look at Finn and Izzy. Izzy's lips were pressed tightly together, and she gave Phae a sympathetic smile.

Finn's hand glided up and down her upper arm. She hadn't realized how cold she was until she felt the warmth of his touch. The caring and kindness gave her courage.

Jeffrey's eyes met her steady gaze, then quickly darted away. He gave Finn a long calculating look. She could see the battle going on in her child. Frowning she tried to find the words to explain.

"Jeffrey, I was married to your father for twenty years. I stood by his side in the darkest moments. I raised you and Kera after he died. I remained a widow for fifteen years." She walked over and put her hand on his shoulder. "I deserve to be happy." She glanced to Kera next. "I'd like both of you to be glad for me. But I don't need your approval to live my life."

Jeffrey looked at her. His expression still held anger and resentment.

She felt like life was being drained from her body. She suddenly felt old and tired. Her eyes filled with tears of defeat. She looked to Kera, hoping to see some understanding. Instead, she saw bitterness and confusion.

She turned back to Finn and shrugged. "I don't know what else to say."

"I think there has been a great deal said. Perhaps you and your children need time to digest everything." He looked from Jeffrey to Kera. "You are both welcome to stay the night."

Dead, cold, empty silence hung in the air. No one moved. No one spoke.

Phae's heart hammered in her chest. Finn's words echoed in her mind. *He is a good man*, she thought.

Phae's voice was flat when she spoke. "Jeff and Kera, please stay the night. I agree with Finn, we need to digest everything that has been said. We can finish talking in the morning."

"No, Mother." Jeffrey's voice was harsh. "You need to decide now. Either we're important enough that you come home with us, or you never see your grandchildren again."

Phae felt herself sway. She grabbed the back of the sofa. "You can't mean that, Jeffrey? Kera, is that how you feel as well?"

Phae couldn't breathe; everything was upside down. She pictured Kaitlin, Mark and Alice in her mind, remembering the times they had played, laughed, and made up silly stories together. She could hear their sweet voices in her mind. She had so many plans, things she wanted to do with them. Things she wanted to teach them. She wanted to take them to the zoo and to see dinosaurs at the museum. She wanted to take them to Sunday school and watch them in the Christmas pageant. She imagined them in school performances. If she wanted to experience those things, she had only one choice, and that was to do what Jeff and Kera wanted.

"Well Mother, what's it going to be?"

Jeffrey's voice sounded far away because her ears were ringing.

# Chapter Thirty-two

Her throat felt like she'd swallowed sandy gravel. Phae swallowed and in a muffled voice replied, "If that's what you want, I'll go with you."

"Phae." She heard the pain in Finn's voice, but she couldn't look at him. Her mind went to how happy he had made her, and guilt shafted through her when she realized all she had done was cause him pain. She wanted to remember his handsome, smiling face, not one filled with contempt at her inability to stand up to her children.

In a soft, painful whisper she said, "Goodbye, Finn. Goodbye, Izzy."

***

Finn watched, stunned, as she turned and started toward the hall.

Jeffrey and Kera were behind her. Desperation to stop this swelled within him. He had to do or say something. As the young man walked by, Finn reached out and touched his shoulder. "Do you have any idea how cruel you are being to your mother?"

Jeffrey shrugged Finn's hand off and kept walking.

Finn looked at Kera, he curled his hands into fists, his voice soft yet pleading. "Doesn't she deserve some happiness?"

Kera looked back at him then lowered her head. "I'm sorry."

Tightness invaded Finn's chest and blood pounded in his temples as he absorbed the turn of events. This is what he had been afraid of—her having to choose between her grandchildren and him.

But he wouldn't do what her children had done. He wouldn't force her to choose. It had to be her decision to take a chance on her own happiness.

Finn heard the front door close and shortly the roar of a car engine. He wanted to walk to the bar and get a drink, but he couldn't move. He was frozen. Somewhere in the distance, he heard a soft cry and then Izzy was hugging him tearfully.

Several minutes passed. His mind was in turmoil and his heart in an uproar. Izzy pulled away from him and sighed. Somehow they found their way to the sofa and sat down.

"Oh Daddy, I'm so sorry for you."

In a lifeless voice, he tried to reassure her. "Don't worry, Izzy. I'll be okay. We have each other and a little one on the way."

They sat in silence. Finn was disgusted with Jeffrey's manipulation of his mother using her Achilles heel. He was only a grandfather in the making and yet he could already relate to what Phae must feel at the prospect of losing her grandchildren.

***

The journey to the ferryboat was quiet. Phae closed her eyes and leaned her head back. The windows were down, and she savored every smell, every brush of the breeze upon her face. She was determined not to let Jeffrey or Kera see her cry, but she had no desire to speak to them. She didn't respond when Kera offered consoling words. "It will be all right once we get you home. The kids have missed you."

Phae was grateful that it was night. The plane was dark. She didn't want to give her children the satisfaction of knowing how much they had hurt her. She tried to sleep but images of Finn pierced her mind and heart.

When they arrived in Wisconsin, she was dazed as she went through baggage claim.

The drive from the airport to home was awkward and silent. She stared out the window and it was like watching her life swoosh away. Emptiness took over her heart. All she wanted was to get away from these two and be alone.

As they turned into the driveway of her home, it looked dark and empty and matched her mood.

"Would you like to stay with me tonight?" Kera asked.

Phae's body stiffened. "No, I prefer to be alone."

"It's barren at your house, and there's no food. I… I just thought you would be more comfortable at my house."

"Well, you thought incorrectly."

She watched the glance between Jeffrey and Kera. Mothers were supposed to love their children unconditionally, but she was so furious she wanted to scream. She jumped out of the car as soon as it stopped in her driveway and made her way to the front door, not bothering to say goodnight.

Once the door closed behind her, Phae dropped her bag and walked to the kitchen. She leaned against the glass door. The backyard was dimly lit by the moon, and she watched as a cloud passed and left the are in darkness. She lowered herself to the floor, hugging her knees and let the grief settle thick and suffocating.

Phae fell asleep on the floor and dreamt of Finn. She felt his arms around her. *"You're cold. Let's get you a blanket."* She shivered and awoke to darkness and quiet. Her head pounded from crying. She stood up and began to see the break of daylight peeping through the clouds.

# Chapter Thirty-three

Several weeks passed, and Phae got back into the routine of watching either Kera's children or Jeffrey's—or sometimes all of them—at Kera's house. Two-year-old Kaitlin loved to look at photos. "Grandma, I want to see pictures," she said one afternoon when they were together.

Phae pulled out her phone. As they scrolled through her images from Italy, Kaitlin would stop and say, "That's you, Grandma," or ask, "Who's your friend?"

As she stared at Finn's smiling face, Phae couldn't control the tears.

"Don't cry, Grandma. Don't be sad," Kaitlin said as she patted her shoulder.

As Phae drove home afterward, her mind filled with thoughts of Finn. Looking at the pictures with Kaitlin had driven home what she'd already known… how much she loved and missed Finn. She felt as if she'd had the life sucked out of her and she couldn't breathe. Now she wondered why she'd allowed her children to issue that ultimatum.

The blare of horns pulled her out of her reverie. She looked up to see several cars swerve away from her. An SUV squealed to a stop inches away from her door.

Her heart pounded in her throat. She felt lightheaded and horrified at her narrow escape. She'd been distracted by thoughts of her children and their unreasonable demand.

She pulled over and stopped the car next to a small park. She needed to pull herself together before she got herself or someone else killed.

A young couple with children caught her eye. The couple walked toward the park holding hands as the kids skipped out in front of them. She felt a stab of envy for something she'd never had—the feeling of being actually connected to a spouse.

The parents were holding hands and talking, and every now and then they would stop and gaze into each other's eyes. He would say something that would make her laugh, and he'd kiss her cheek. She longed to feel that connection with Finn.

She'd considered it briefly in Rome and had begun to believe she could have it. She shivered, feeling lonely. Tears dripped down her cheek, and she thought about how Finn had made her laugh and how he would pull her into an embrace. She'd made the wrong decision leaving him behind to give into the demands of her children, and she wanted a second chance.

Phae heard a cry and saw the young boy of around five years old hanging upside down on the swing. The father ran to pull him off. Phae was expecting the father to yell and berate the child, and the mother. She was surprised when the man simply removed the child and righted him, and then knelt and explained how the boy could have gotten hurt. When the mother joined the father and son, the man put his arm around her to comfort her as well.

A similar incident had happened when Phae's children were young, only George had scolded Jeffrey so loudly that a crowd gathered to witness it. When she had approached to quiet things down George yelled at her, blaming her for Jeffrey's unruliness. He had gotten so verbally abusive that another man had come over to calm him down. They had left the park and, as soon as they were home and the kids in their room, George lit into her, accusing her of embarrassing him in public.

She wanted to huddle in a ball and make the pain go away, but she now saw where she'd failed her children. George had been so hard on them, yelling and belittling them, that she had jumped through hoops to keep the peace and to run interference for them. She'd felt guilty because George treated them badly so she had made up for it by giving them anything they wanted and doing everything they asked. Her goal had been to give them joy and let them be children, but she'd spoiled them and made them selfish.

Her thoughts turned to Jeffrey. He was a single parent and needed help with his daughter when he had her. She saw so much of George in him that she worried about what kind of father he would become. She could understand why Tracy had left him, and she wished she'd had Tracy's courage. Maybe then her children would have turned out differently.

Kera seemed to be happy, but was afraid of letting her go. It occurred to Phae that perhaps it wasn't so much fear of letting her go, as it was that Kera wanted to keep her brother happy. Kera was the peacemaker, always trying to fix things. Phae shook her head realizing that was exactly what she herself had done.

No wonder her children had grown up expecting her to capitulate to everything they wanted. She had failed to set boundaries and expectations, but that still left her with the question of what she was going to do about it. She wanted a second chance at love and family, but she had to decide whether she could accept it if Jeff and Kera upheld the threat of denying her access to her grandchildren. Was she willing to give up seeing them all in order to build a life with Finn?

Phae rubbed her temples as she thought about the repercussions of the decision. What could they do, get a court order against her? She could go to their school for special events and to their activities. They couldn't have her thrown out of public places.

Then she began wondering what her children would tell the kids. There wouldn't be a painless way of explaining why they didn't see her anymore, and she couldn't imagine Kera and Jeffrey doing something that would hurt their children. That would hurt them as well, just as much as it would hurt the little ones.

The more Phae thought about it, the more she thought they were bluffing. She wavered. Could she truly be happy if she didn't see her children and grandchildren? She questioned herself about the void in her heart. Yes, there would be Izzy and the new baby, but they would be reminders of what she had left behind.

The more she thought about the bond she had with her children, the more convinced she became that the separation wouldn't last long. Her children might be selfish, but they were not mean-spirited. The ultimatum was the equivalent to a child's temper tantrum. She hadn't caved to their tantrums when they were children, and she was not going to cave now. She needed to call their bluff.

Phae wanted to believe that, eventually, they could all be one happy family. Her kids would get to know Finn and see what a good man he was.

She shook her head and scolded herself, realizing it didn't matter how good a man he was. That was not the issue.

She needed to get real and look at the situation for what it was. Her children were selfish. She'd been so afraid of hurting them that she'd allowed them to run her life.

They were grown adults, and a little reality check was in order. She was their mother, and she was entitled to her own life, separate from theirs. She needed to quit tiptoeing around them and stand up for herself. If they had to give up some "conveniences" like an on-call babysitter, gofer, cook, and financial aid assistant, then it was their choice.

She sighed, realizing how much they had used her, but she was to blame too. She had allowed it to continue.

If they could only see that her happiness would benefit them as well. She knew Kera had always wanted a big family. As old as he was, Jeffrey still needed a male role model. She knew it wouldn't be easy and that it would take lots of work, but she hoped they would try, because if they didn't, then she would have to let go. This was her chance to have the loving, supportive relationship she'd always longed for.

She felt confident for the first time since she'd come home from Spain. She knew what she had to do and wanted to waste no time. She felt a surge of energy when she arrived at her house. She went about straightening the rooms and baked a coffeecake. While it was in the oven, she called her daughter.

"Kera, I am calling a family meeting. Will you and David come over this evening around seven-thirty?

There was silence before Kera spoke. "Okay… Do you want me to bring the children?"

Phae thought for a moment. The conversation might get ugly, and she didn't want her grandchildren to overhear an argument about them. "No. You'll need to get a sitter."

"Is everything okay, Mom? What's going on?"

"I'll discuss it this evening."

She called Jeffrey, but got his voicemail and left him a message. She stared at the phone. She wanted to call Finn as well. She needed him, but she also needed to do this on her own, for herself.

At seven-thirty they hadn't arrived, so she began pacing around the living room. She couldn't help but think it was just like them to be late. Everything had to be on their terms and in their timeframe. Resentment formed in her mind.

She heard the kitchen door open. "Kera, Jeffrey is that you?"

"Yes, Mom. We're here."

"Good. I made coffee and a cake if anyone would like some." She glanced at them and noticed that they were waiting for her to serve it. They stood there not moving. She cut herself a piece and poured coffee for herself.

Jeffrey started to reach out to pick up the plate and cup. Phae quickly snatched both items. "Help yourselves, and bring it in the living room."

Phae felt strange and a little rude not to serve them first. But this would be a baby step to setting new ground rules. This wasn't a social visit. She was going to create boundaries of her own, and it wasn't going to be pleasant.

Phae sat in the high-backed Victorian chair. While she waited, she gave herself a mental pep talk. Her hands trembled, and her throat felt as if it was closing up. She sipped the coffee to ease her nausea.

David and Kera sat on the sofa, and Jeffrey chose the chair across from her. She laughed to herself, thinking the lines had been drawn. How appropriate, since she'd be setting new boundaries.

When they were all settled, David asked, "How was your trip, Phae? I haven't seen you since you got back."

"It was lovely." She glanced at Kera, and it occurred to her that her daughter must not have mentioned anything to him about the reason for her returning home. "I'm sorry it was cut short."

She stared at Kera's lowered head. There was a part of Phae that sympathized with Kera, but another, stronger part needed to make it clear she would fight for what she wanted.

"My trip being cut short is what I brought you all here to discuss."

Phae wondered if everyone could hear her heart thumping. Now that the words were out and the first line drawn, she would have to hold her ground. Her knees were shaking, and she was thankful she was seated.

"First, Kera and Jeffrey, I apologize for not being more forthcoming regarding Finn."

"Excuse me, who is Finn?" David asked.

Phae saw him give Kera a puzzled look.

"Really, Mother. We caught the two of you in a passionate kiss." Jeffrey sneered.

Phae felt her temperature rising but told herself to remain calm. "I'm not a sixteen year old that you 'caught' doing anything. You make it sound like I was behaving immorally. I've been a widow for fifteen years. I don't believe I need to ask anyone's permission to kiss, or, for that matter, to do anything else."

"I'm confused. What is going on here?" David queried.

"What is going on here, David, is that my adult children issued me an ultimatum. Come home or never see my grandchildren again."

David turned to look at Kera, his eyes wide, his mouth open. He pursed lips and shook his head. "Phae, I'm so sorry. I didn't know anything about this."

"I gathered that was the case when you asked about my trip." Phae let out a big sigh. "I have realized I made a wrong decision and that it was a knee jerk reaction." She waited for their reactions. "I want you to understand why." She stood and began to pace.

Jeffrey started to say something.

"No, Jeffrey. I need you to listen. Grant me that courtesy, please." She knew her voice sounded sharp. She intended to come across with the message that she was in control. She was not going to let them change the direction of the conversation.

Jeffrey sat back in his chair and crossed one leg over his knee. He spread his arms and waved his hands, indicting she should continue. He wore a know-it-all-expression that reminded her of the one George had used when he'd cornered her and wanted to fight. She contained the urge to pummel her son, vowing that she'd never let him manipulate her like that again.

"When I left for Spain, my intention was to see the sights that I had dreamt of seeing. I wanted time to think about what I still want out of the rest of my life, which could be another day or another twenty years."

"Mom, don't talk like that."

"Why, Kera? Because it makes you uncomfortable? It's a fact that none of us knows when it will be our time. But I want to live my life to the fullest until then. Until I met Finn, I hadn't realized how much I missed being a woman. How much I missed seeing a man's eyes light up when I entered a room. Like David's do when he sees you."

Phae saw Kera and David exchange a look. Jeffrey's posture became more humble.

"I wasn't looking for a relationship," she continued. "But it happened. We talked and listened to each other." An image of Finn flashed through her mind. She felt a stab of shame at how she had left him. He'd deserved so much better.

"I shouldn't have left Finn the way I did. Since I've been back here, I've realized that I need to set better boundaries with the two of you."

She observed their confused expressions, but the image of Finn gave her courage to continue. "I jumped through hoops for your father to keep the peace. Then I over-compensated for your dad's harshness by giving the two of you everything you wanted, without thought of how I was doing you a disservice.

"Both of you have your own lives. You have children to raise, and when they are grown, you will want to do the things you missed out on. Maybe then you will understand, but whether you do or not, I'm done jumping through hoops to please other people. I have the right to live my own life, to make my own decisions, to see who I want to see. I have made the decision to call Finn and see if he would like to see me again."

Kera and Jeffrey frowned. David smiled at her and patted Kera's hand. Her heart thumped, and she felt weak kneed and returned to her chair.

"I'm sorry for going along with the ultimatum."

Kera looked over at Jeffrey. "We talked yesterday over lunch, and I realized that it was wrong and that we were hasty."

Phae gritted her teeth as the anger sizzled within her.

"You are not my parents, and I don't need your approval. I want your acceptance and blessing. But if I don't have it, I'm not going to change my mind."

She looked from one to the other. "Do you have any idea how your actions affected the most beautiful time of my life?"

She knew she was making progress when she saw their heads drop in shame, but she had to make it clear. "I deserve happiness just as both of you do. I don't stand in your way and give you ultimatums when you want to do something that I don't think is a good idea." She let her voice fall. "It's time for this family to forget the past and rebuild a new happier life for all of us."

Her anger was subsiding and her confidence growing with each tick of the hour. "I'm not going to let you manipulate me again," she warned.

The clocked chimed eight times. When it stopped, Phae looked up. "If you have anything else to say about my relationship with Finn, say it now. But it will not change my mind about contacting him."

Phae waited. When no one spoke, she said, "Fine. Now if you will excuse me, I have a phone call to make."

Jeffrey rose to leave. He came over to where she was sitting and bent to give her a kiss on the cheek. "I'm sorry, Mom."

Tears welled in her eyes. She loved her children, and she wanted to accept their apologies but they had really hurt her.

However, this was a start.

"I know you are. I'm to blame for letting it happen, but I won't be doing that again. She raised her hand and gently patted his cheek. "Goodnight."

"Mom," Kera said. "I'd like to stay and be here for you after your phone call."

Phae looked at her daughter, wondering what she was up to.

"To be your support, Mom. Good or bad news."

She patted Kera's arm. "I appreciate that, darling, but this is a private matter, and I would prefer to be alone. Thank you for your thoughtfulness." She gave her daughter a smile. "Besides, your children are waiting for the two of you."

Phae rose, hugged her daughter and David, and walked them to the door. She could feel Kera's hesitancy. "I'll be fine," she promised.

After they left, Phae picked up the dishes and loaded the dishwasher, her mind in disarray. What was she going to say to Finn? She glanced at the clock and calculated the time difference.

It would be about three in the morning in Spain. She went outside and gazed up at the moon. It wasn't nearly as bright as the Mallorca moon. The sky was black, but it lacked the glow of the stars that she and Finn had seen when they were in Rome.

She toyed with the idea of calling him. She didn't want to wake him, but she did want to speak to him urgently. She studied her phone as if looking for it to tell her what to do. Her fingers felt numb as she tapped out a text message. "Please call me."

# Chapter Thirty-four

Finn had arrived in Chicago at eight-thirty P.M. He couldn't get Phae out of his mind. He wanted to give her time to… *What*, he wondered. *Miss him?* He scoffed at himself. For the last month, he had been on a rollercoaster ride. One minute angry with her for the way she had left, the next understanding why it had been impossible for her to risk never seeing her grandchildren again. Then he would catch himself seeking her out in the house, only to remember she was gone.

The ache for Phae was worse than when his wife had died. There had been comfort in knowing his wife no longer suffered. With Phae, it had been a rejection. What made it worse was that he knew she had loved him and thrown it away. He shook his head and thought of the anguish she must have felt because of her selfish children.

His emotions subsided as he walked to his car in the airport parking lot. Even while he admonished himself for being a fool, he kept telling himself there had to be a way to fix this.

He felt his cell phone vibrate as he unlocked the trunk. He threw his bag inside then climbed in the car and pulled out his phone.

He read the words over and over again, wondering if something was wrong that had caused her to reach out. He was afraid to hope that she wanted to return to their relationship. He put his head against the headrest and closed his eyes. He could call her, but that seemed impersonal, somehow. He wouldn't be able to touch her or see her facial expressions over the phone. If instead he drove to Glendale, he'd be there in two hours.

When she had left him, there had been no time for a proper goodbye. He had made it easy for her to leave. He rubbed his chin. *Not this time,* he thought. This time, he wanted a chance to convince her to come back. If he was going to talk to her, it had to be face to face.

He replied to her message: "Can't talk now. Talk later." Then he started the car and headed north.

*****

Phae reread the text, thankful that he had at least acknowledged her message but disappointed that he hadn't been able to speak to her right then. It puzzled her that he hadn't been asleep. Perhaps she had woken him. Or maybe he was on a business call; she knew he worked all hours of the day and night. Then the thought struck her that perhaps he didn't want to talk to her, and this was his way of putting her off.

Nausea rose in her stomach at the thought that she might have lost him for good. How could she have been so stupid? She turned on the TV to alleviate the silence as she waited for Finn to call.

She dozed off, but somewhere, mingled among the shadowy images of a dream she heard the chime of a doorbell. Shaking off her drowsiness, she woke up and listened. It definitely was the doorbell, but who would be at her door at this hour of the night.

"Who's there?" she called.

There was no answer for a second. Alarm bubbled up in her throat.

"You said you wanted me to call you."

Her hand flew to her chest in surprise. She couldn't believe Finn was actually here. Tears of happiness filled her eyes. A multitude of emotions from happiness to fear and dread flooded through her. She couldn't seem to make herself move. It was as if she were glued to the floor.

Drawing in a deep breath, she forced her feet to move and walked to the door. Joy surged through her, and she felt as if she were floating.

Almost ripping the door from its hinges, she swung it open and stared at him wide eyed for two full seconds before she went into his arms.

His muscles tensed under her touch, and she stepped back. "Please, come in. Oh, my gosh, I can't believe you're here." A sudden, blinding, intense need for him overtook her and she wrapped her hand around his neck and brought his lips to hers. She wanted to lean into the safety of his reassurance. Need and desire bubbled up and overflowed.

Finally, they eased apart. When Finn met her gaze, Phae saw wariness. She put her arm around his waist and led him to the sofa. "You're probably wondering why I called you."

He didn't say anything, but he squeezed her hand to encourage her to continue.

A lump formed in her throat. "I owe you an apology for the way I left." She paused hoping he would say something.

***

Finn didn't want to make this easy for her. She had to decide once and for all whether she wanted him or not. "I'm listening." He glanced at Phae's hand locked in his. He felt it tremble.

"I've been miserable without you. I told the kids tonight that I was going to call you and… ask if you would take me back…"

Finn could see the look of concern etched on her face. He let go of her hand, stood up and walked to the fireplace. "Take you back how, Phae?" He stopped. "As my caretaker and decorator?"

He saw her shoulders slump. Her face paled, and she stumbled back a step. "I'm so sorry, Finn. Please forgive me."

In his heart, he knew he wanted nothing more than to take her back, forgive, and begin sharing a life together.

"You haven't answered my question, Phae."

She bit her bottom lip as she always did when she was struggling to express herself.

"I asked you a question the night you left me. You never gave me an answer." He saw the look of hope that emerged in her eyes. He swallowed and his eyes locked on hers waiting for her to speak.

"Finn Callahan, I would like to come back as your lover, and your wife if the offer is still open."

He wanted to believe her. The evening she had left him flashed before his eyes as he remembered how she had caved in without putting up a fight. How could he be sure she wouldn't let her children manipulate her again? "What about the next time your kids give you an ultimatum?"

Finn stared only at her as she walked over to him. "I told them I don't need their approval. I deserve happiness and the chance to be with the man I love." She lowered her head. "I realized I was as much to blame as they were. I was afraid to stand up for myself." She looked up at him. "I told them I will not let them manipulate me anymore, and I meant that." She placed her hand in his. "You give me strength and courage, and I love you."

***

Phae held her breath, waiting for him to say something. When there wasn't a response, she thought about what else she could add. "I'll buy you a hot tub."

She loved the sound of laughter that bubbled up from deep in his chest and the warmth of his arms that came around her and pulled her against him as he nibbled at her neck. "I love you, Finn. Can you forgive me… and my children?"

"I forgive you as long as we don't have to wait long to get married." He held her close, and she didn't want him to let go. "As for your children, I anticipated it would be a shock for them. I understand where they are coming from."

"I don't deserve you."

Finn placed his fingers over her lips. "You deserve happiness and love, and I want to be the one to give them to you."

# Epilogue

*Eight months later*

Phae had to pinch herself to make sure she wasn't dreaming. As they watched their wedding video, her heart swelled with love and joy. What a whirlwind the past year had been.

Phae snuggled deeper into Finn's arms. She felt his lips caress her temple. "What a beautiful and chaotic day."

Finn chuckled. "I got married and became a grandfather in the same day."

"At least the baby decided to wait until the ceremony was over before her arrival."

When the video concluded, Phae stood. "It will be easy for you to remember our anniversary."

"Like I could ever forget." He pulled her to his lap. "It has been a crazy year, but I wouldn't change a moment of it."

"Neither would I." Phae rested her head on Finn's shoulder as the memories came to mind. They'd found a house that put them halfway between all the kids. They'd finished the renovations on the villa and planned two weddings. And… the birth of Elizabeth Phae, lovingly called "Lizzy."

She had been particularly proud of her children, who had embraced Izzy and Luke with open arms. Jeffrey and Finn had even started playing golf.

"What time are the troops descending on us?" Finn asked.

"Oh, my gosh. I forgot! They will be here any minute," she said as the doorbell sounded.

Phae opened the door, and Kera and Jeffrey's children ran in. "Grandpa, Grandpa!" they shouted.

Luke and Izzy were right behind Jeffrey and Kera and her husband, David. Little Lizzy was crying, and Phae reached out to take her. She walked into the living room to see Finn juggling three children on his lap.

Laughter and mayhem filled the house, and all Phae could think was, *My cup runneth over.*

*The End*

# About the Author

Carol Schoenig used to joke with co-workers that when she retired she was going to sit on a beach and write scintillating romance novels.

She now spends time with her two grown sons and five grandchildren. She reads, sews and sings.

She believes you're never too old to pursue your dreams.

AuthorCarolSchoenig@gmail.com

https://caschoenig.wixsite.com/my-site-1